徐薇英文UP學堂
親子共學系列 5

徐薇老師精彩解析MP3
（附教學光碟、綜合練習題）

讓你一聽就懂，聽完就會！

精選

全民英檢初級
60組英聽題型解析

300題英檢
初級聽力模擬

《親子共學系列》緣起

教了二十多年的英文，我真的認為，爸媽才是孩子學好英文最重要的啟蒙老師。

教過數萬名國、高中學生，我發現班上英文程度好的孩子，都有一個共通的特點，就是他們的爸媽從小就很重視培養孩子的英文實力。除了固定送孩子上兒童美語班外，還會在家創造英文學習環境，有的爸媽會每天陪孩子讀英文讀本、聽英文 CD；有的會陪孩子看英文教學卡通；還有的爸媽會在家設定固定時段的 No Chinese Time，這段時間裡全家都必須講英文。

在父母的陪伴下，英文成為孩子日常生活的一部分，孩子對英文的接受度就會高，效果自然就好，而這樣打下的基礎，讓孩子對自己的英文能力更有自信，也就更想要把英文學好，於是，孩子的英文學習走向了良性循環，英文程度愈來愈好也是理所當然的事。

另外，有些家長，從小就送孩子上兒童美語，接著上國、高中文理補習班，本身也非常關心孩子們的英文，但自己陪伴的時間較少，這些同學表現就不如上面的同學，考大學英文成績約為中上程度，最差的是，家長從小比較不關心孩子的英文教育，那麼，這些同學，到了高中，大學時就比較容易放棄英文，**因此，可以說，在小孩 6-12 歲英文學習的關鍵期，家長越是重視，孩子們長大以後，英文程度越好。**

我認為，小學是奠定孩子英文基礎最重要的時機，但在這個階段中，我也知道很多有心的家長，很想幫孩子創造學英文的環境，卻常苦於找不到適合的教材、覺得沒有時間、或是對自己的英文沒有信心，讓孩子白白錯失了英文打底的最佳時機，這也正是我要推出親子共學系列的原因。

在這套系列書中，我們融入了英文學程的概念，將英文元素設計成一堂堂完整的課程，每堂課都有我的詳細解說，爸媽們不用在費心尋找教材的同時，還要擔心自己英文程度不夠好、不會教的問題，只要每天或每週花三十分鐘的時間，陪著孩子一起聽我的教學，再利用書裡的檢測試題做測驗，隨時就能知道孩子的學習狀況和理解程度，不記得的地方還可以一聽再聽，加強印象。

我們現已推出了《英單 1500 字 Starter（上）、（下）》兩冊、《徐薇老師教 KK》、《初級片語 Starter 300》以及《初級聽力 Starter》，接下來還有文法課程套書及初級英檢模擬測驗等親子共學系列套書，要為爸媽們提供最有效、有趣而且最紮實的英文教學素材。

最重要的是，有了您的陪伴，孩子就不會覺得無聊孤單，能和爸媽一起學有趣的英文，也就更有持續學習的動力，基礎就能打得更紮實，未來學英文當然更有自信。

《親子共學系列》將和您一起，讓孩子的英文學習如虎添翼！

徐薇

初級聽力
Starter

目錄 contents

序言 preface

「國中會考加考英聽！」
斗大的新聞標題，讓你擔心不已嗎？
不用怕！有徐薇老師就搞定了！

很多學習者學了兩、三年英文，會讀也會寫，但一聽到英文聽力題，就嚇得不知如何反應；或是一聽到老外說話就老是狀況外，只能站在原地傻傻發呆。

其實，學好聽力不難，每天只要三分鐘，跟著徐薇老師練英聽最輕鬆。

本書依照全民英檢聽力測驗題型分類，包括：「看圖辨義」、「問答」、「對話」及「短文聽解」四大類，每種題型還依最常出現的題目走向做歸納整理，不論是看鐘錶、比較價格還是高難度的廣播短文，每個小分類都有徐薇老師親自講解聽題重點和單字解析，讓您一聽到題目就知道答案在哪裡。

聽完徐薇老師的講解後，還可以立即進行隨堂練習，試試自己是否有抓到聽題技巧；整個題型練完後還有綜合挑戰題，超過三百道英聽測驗練習，在家就可天天模擬、天天聽考，不論是全民英檢初級、國中會考還是各式大、小型英文考試，讓你怎麼考都考不倒！

跟著徐薇老師學英聽，不僅教你各種英聽解題密技，還能邊聽邊練，讓你的英聽功力迅速UP！UP！UP！

頁面說明

徐薇老師親自解說英聽答題技巧，英聽考試難不倒！

Part 1 看圖辨義

Part 2 問答題

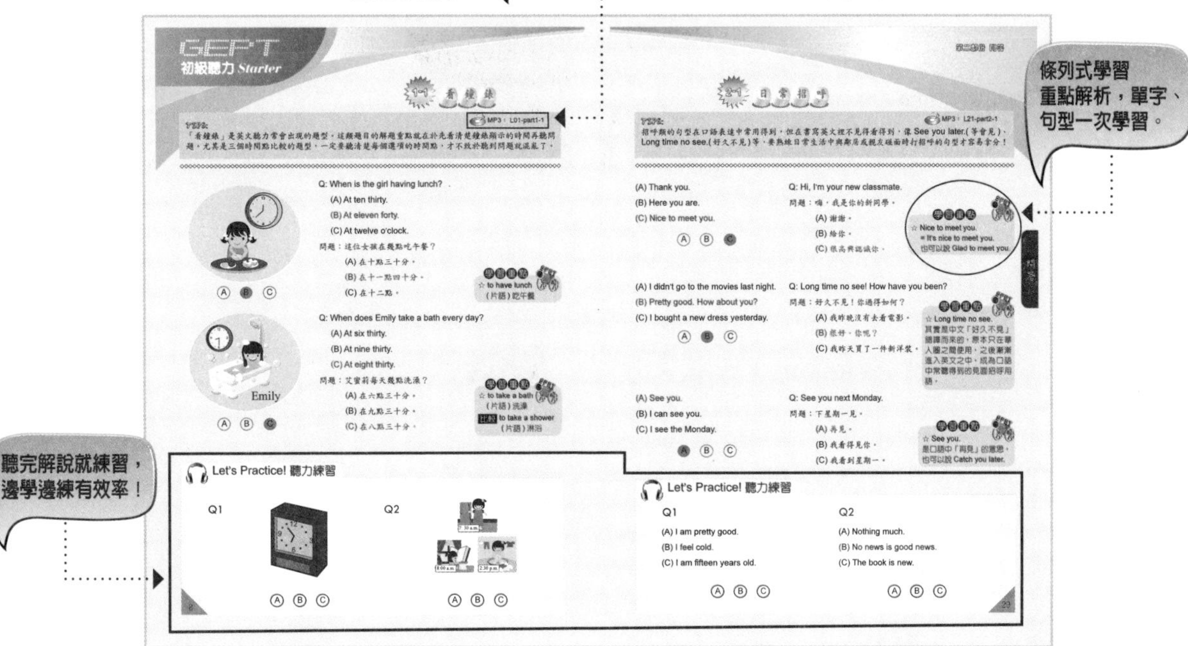

Part 3 對話題

Part 4 短文聽解

題目內容中、英文完整條列，一看就懂，一聽就會。

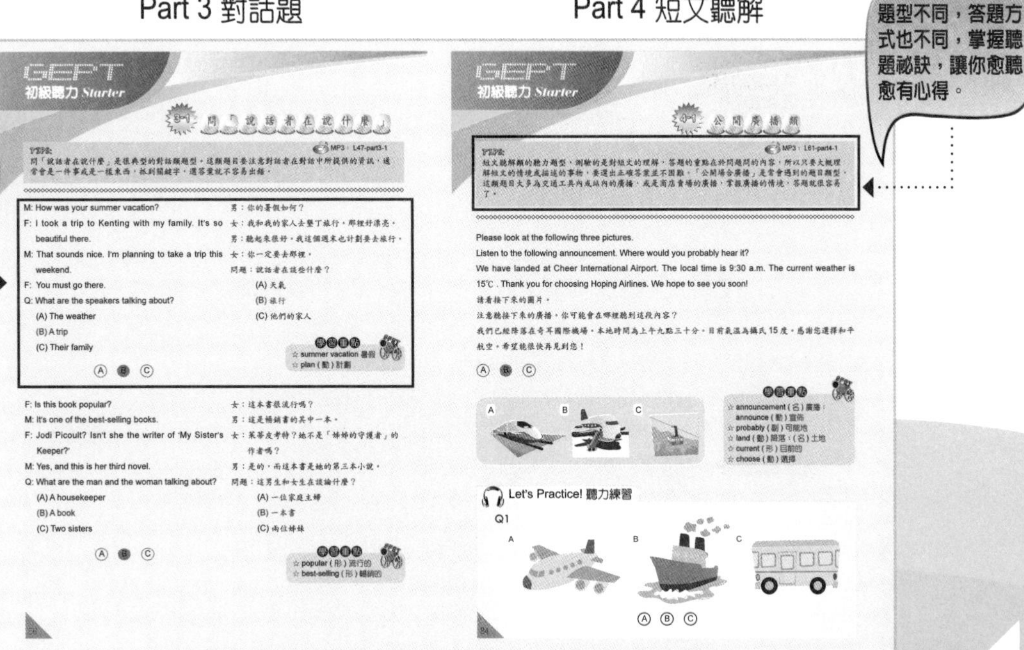

初級聽力
Starter

頁面說明

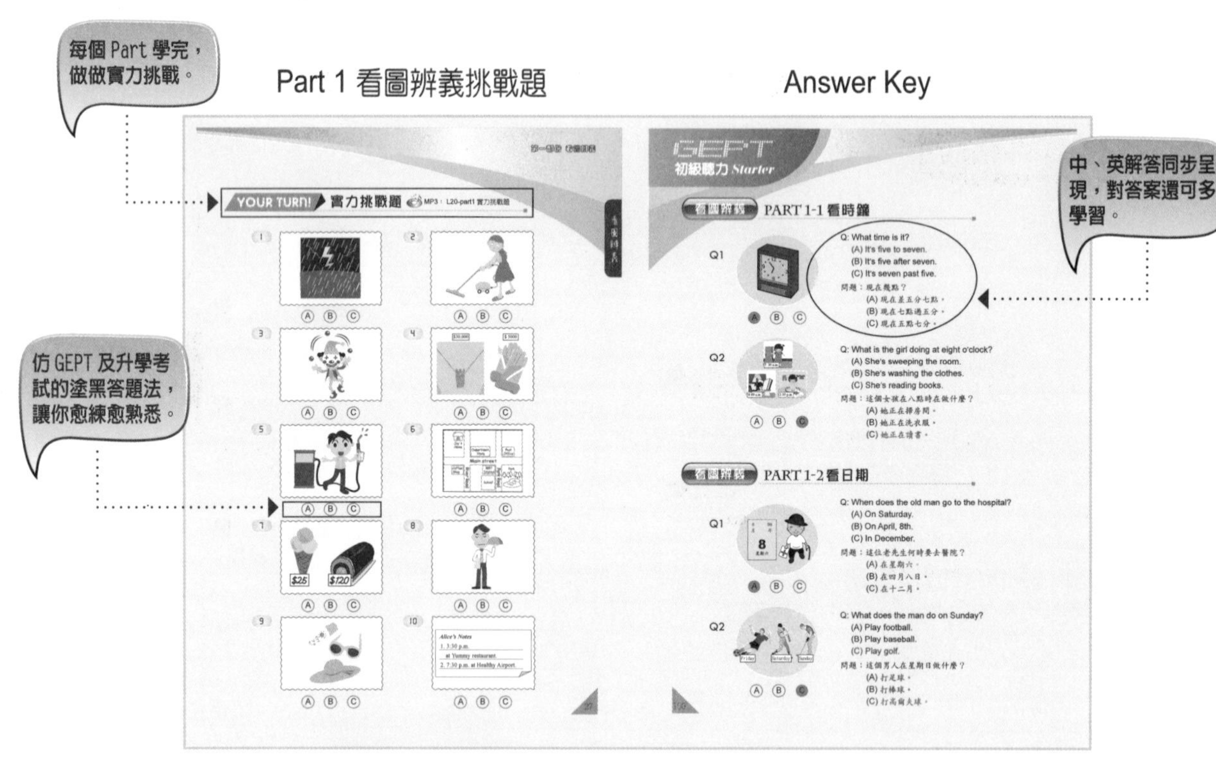

每個 Part 學完，做做實力挑戰。
Part 1 看圖辨義挑戰題
Answer Key
YOUR TURN! 實力挑戰題
仿 GEPT 及升學考試的塗黑答題法，讓你愈練愈熟悉。
中、英解答同步呈現，對答案還可多學習。
GEPT 初級聽力 Starter
PART 1-1 看時鐘
Q: What time is it?
(A) It's five to seven.
(B) It's five after seven.
(C) It's seven past five.
Q: What is the girl doing at eight o'clock?
(A) She's sweeping the room.
(B) She's washing the clothes.
(C) She's reading books.
PART 1-2 看日期
Q: When does the old man go to the hospital?
(A) On Saturday.
(B) On April, 8th.
(C) In December.
Q: What does the man do on Sunday?
(A) Play football.
(B) Play baseball.
(C) Play golf.

學習成果測驗

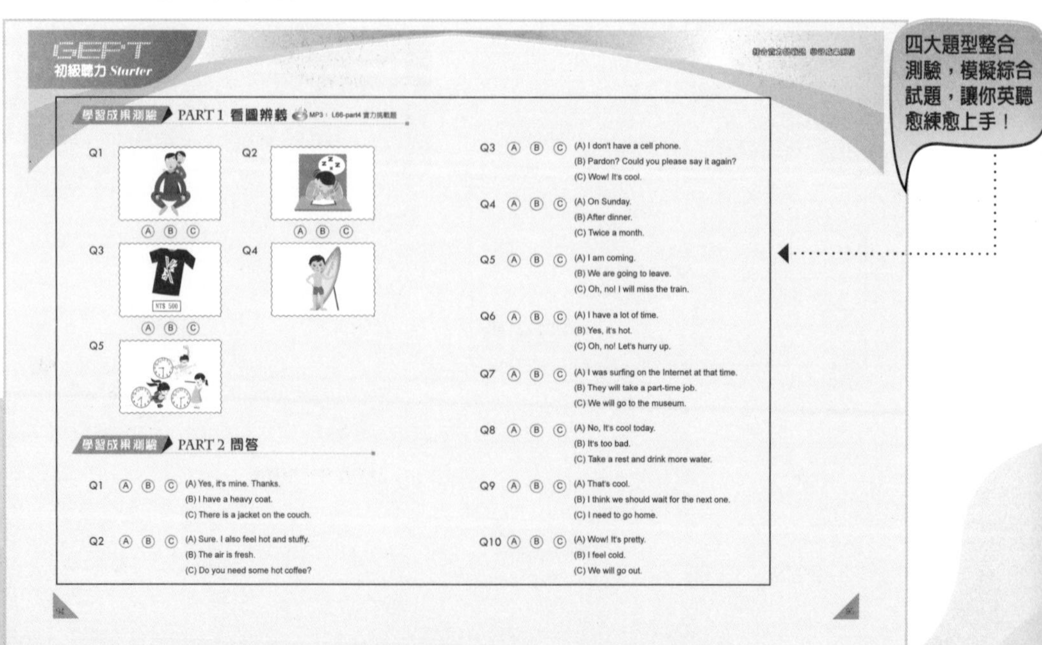

GEPT 初級聽力 Starter
學習成果測驗 PART 1 看圖辨義
學習成果測驗 PART 2 問答
Q1 (A) Yes, it's mine. Thanks. (B) I have a heavy coat. (C) There is a jacket on the couch.
Q2 (A) Sure. I also feel hot and stuffy. (B) The air is fresh. (C) Do you need some hot coffee?
Q3 (A) I don't have a cell phone. (B) Pardon? Could you please say it again? (C) Wow! It's cool.
Q4 (A) On Sunday. (B) After dinner. (C) Twice a month.
Q5 (A) I am coming. (B) We are going to leave. (C) Oh, no! I will miss the train.
Q6 (A) I have a lot of time. (B) Yes, it's hot. (C) Oh, no! Let's hurry up.
Q7 (A) I was surfing on the Internet at that time. (B) They will take a part-time job. (C) We will go to the museum.
Q8 (A) No, It's cool today. (B) It's too bad. (C) Take a rest and drink more water.
Q9 (A) That's cool. (B) I think we should wait for the next one. (C) I need to go home.
Q10 (A) Wow! It's pretty. (B) I feel cold. (C) We will go out.
四大題型整合測驗，模擬綜合試題，讓你英聽愈練愈上手！

GEPT 初級聽力 Starter

第一部份 看圖辨義

看圖辨義的題型主要是測驗考生對圖片敘述的理解能力，答題關鍵在於聽清楚選項各是什麼，才能找到符合圖片的選項。

範例題： What are they doing?

(A) They're playing chess.

(B) They're playing basketball.

(C) They're playing the guitar.

正確答案為 (A)

1-1 看鐘錶

TIPS:

MP3：L01-part1-1

「看鐘錶」是英文聽力常會出現的題型。這類題目的解題重點就在於先看清楚鐘錶顯示的時間再聽問題。尤其是三個時間點比較的題型，一定要聽清楚每個選項的時間點，才不致於聽到問題就混亂了。

Q: When is the girl having lunch?

(A) At ten thirty.

(B) At eleven forty.

(C) At twelve o'clock.

問題：這位女孩在幾點吃午餐？

(A) 在十點三十分。

(B) 在十一點四十分。

(C) 在十二點。

學習重點

☆ to have lunch
（片語）吃午餐

Ⓐ  

Q: When does Emily take a bath every day?

(A) At six thirty.

(B) At nine thirty.

(C) At eight thirty.

問題：艾蜜莉每天幾點洗澡？

(A) 在六點三十分。

(B) 在九點三十分。

(C) 在八點三十分。

學習重點

☆ to take a bath
（片語）洗澡

比較 to take a shower
（片語）淋浴

Let's Practice! 聽力練習

Q1

Q2

MP3： L02-part1-2

TIPS:
看月曆或聽日期的題型，最容易混淆的就是 day 與 date 沒聽清楚。What day 是指「星期幾」，而 What date 則是指「幾月幾日」，掌握這個重點才不會容易答錯哦！

Q: What is the date today?

(A) It's the twelfth of November.

(B) It's Friday.

(C) It's the thirteenth of December.

問題：今天是日期是？

(A) 今天是十一月十二日。

(B) 今天是星期五。

(C) 今天是十二月十三日。

☆ date (名) 日期
☆ November (名) 十一月
☆ December (名) 十二月

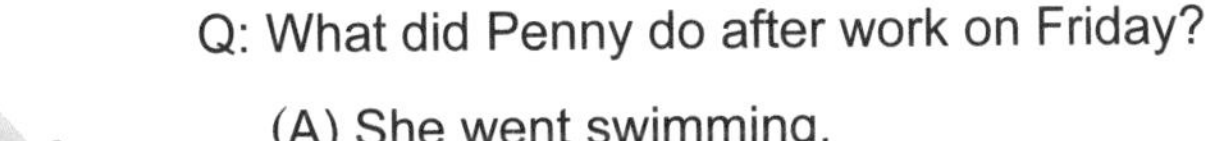

Q: What did Penny do after work on Friday?

(A) She went swimming.

(B) She took a hot spring bath.

(C) She played golf.

Wednesday Thursday Friday

Ⓐ Ⓑ Ⓒ

問題：潘妮星期五下班後做了什麼？

(A) 她去游泳。

(B) 她去泡溫泉。

(C) 她打高爾夫球。

Let's Practice! 聽力練習

Q1

Q2

TIPS:

MP3： L03-part1-3

問天氣的題型比較容易混淆的是兩天以上的氣候比較，聽題目的時候聽清楚是「星期幾」，就不會答錯了哦！

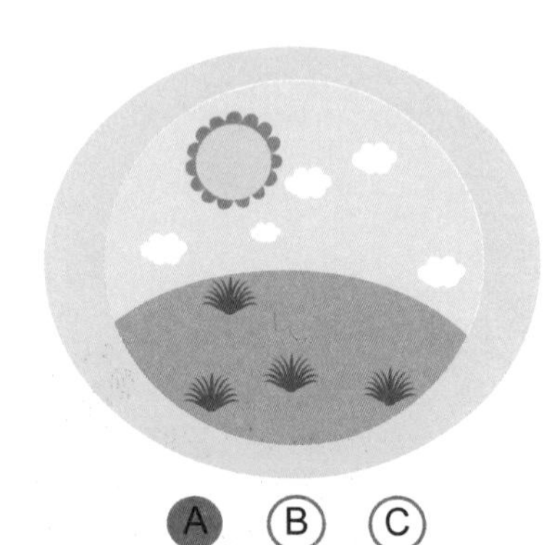

Q: How's the weather?

(A) It's sunny.

(B) It's raining.

(C) It's snowing.

問題：現在天氣如何？

(A) 現在是晴天。

(B) 現在正在下雨。

(C) 現在正在下雪

☆ weather (名) 天氣

比較 climate (名) 氣候

Ⓐ Ⓑ Ⓒ

Friday

Saturday Sunday

Q: How is the weather on Sunday?

(A) It's cloudy.

(B) It's windy.

(C) It's rainy.

問題：星期天的天氣如何？

(A) 陰天。

(B) 風很大。

(C) 下雨天。

☆ cloudy (形) 多雲的

☆ windy (形) 風大的

☆ rainy (形) 多雨的

Ⓐ Ⓑ Ⓒ

Let's Practice! 聽力練習

Q1

  Ⓒ

Q2

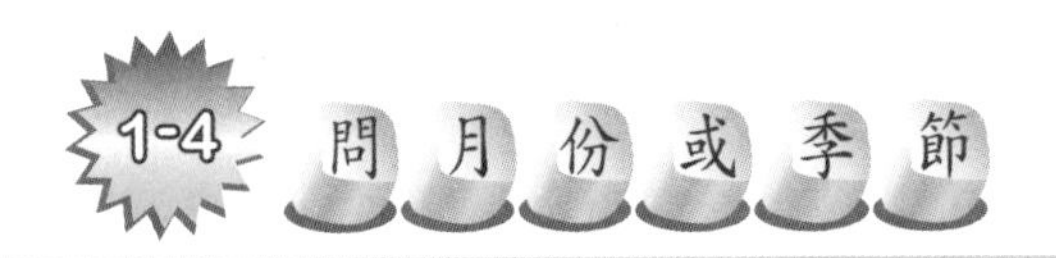

1-4 問月份或季節

MP3： L04-part1-4

TIPS:
問季節時會遇到答案選項裡有節日，即使是在圖片所顯示的季節裡的節日，也要小心題目問的是節日、月份還是季節，不要掉進題目的陷阱裡。

Ⓐ Ⓑ Ⓒ

Q: What season is it?

(A) It's autumn.

(B) It's Christmas.

(C) It's winter.

問題：這是什麼季節？

(A) 這是秋天。

(B) 這是聖誕節。

(C) 這是冬天。

學習重點

☆ autumn（名）秋天
比較 fall（名）秋天
（動）掉落
☆ Christmas（名）聖誕節
☆ winter（名）冬天

Q: What festival is it?

(A) Christmas

(B) Moon Festival

(C) Dragon Boat Festival.

問題：這是什麼節日？

(A) 聖誕節。

(B) 中秋節。

(C) 端午節。

學習重點

☆ festival（名）慶典；節日
比較 holiday（名）假日
☆ Moon Festival
（片語）月亮節＝中秋節
☆ Dragon Boat Festival
（片語）龍舟節＝端午節

Let's Practice! 聽力練習

Q1

Ⓐ Ⓑ Ⓒ

Q2

Ⓐ Ⓑ Ⓒ

TIPS: MP3： L05-part1-5

問數量的題型，常會以 How many 的問句開頭，通常只要數出數量、聽清楚選項就可以拿分；但也有混合式的題型，如：不同種類的兩、三項物品各有兩、三個，結果問題問的不是單一項目的數量，而是物品的項目有幾個；或是選項裡的敘述與圖片內容相符，但卻與題目的問題沒有關係，所以聽題目時一定要小心。

Ⓐ Ⓑ Ⓒ

Q: How many children are there in the park?

(A) There are four children in the park.

(B) There are five children in the park.

(C) There are ten children in the park.

問題：公園裡有幾個小孩？

(A) 公園裡有四個小孩。

(B) 公園裡有五個小孩。

(C) 公園裡有十個小孩。

☆ children (名) 小孩 (複數)

Ⓐ Ⓑ Ⓒ

Q: How many people are there in the picture?

(A) They take a trip to Paris.

(B) They are taking a picture.

(C) There are three people in the picture.

問題：圖片裡有幾個人？

(A) 他們去巴黎旅遊。

(B) 他們正在拍照。

(C) 圖片裡有三個人。

☆ to take a trip
(片語) 旅遊

☆ to take a picture
(片語) 拍照

Let's Practice! 聽力練習

Q1

Ⓐ Ⓑ Ⓒ

Q2

Ⓐ Ⓑ Ⓒ

1-6 問價格

MP3： L06-part1-6

TIPS:

問價格或比價格的題型，一定會同時有兩項以上的物品標價。如果問的是東西的價格，就要注意選項中唸出的數字是否與圖片相符；若題目是問何者為真、或何者有誤，就要注意選項中比較級句子裡較貴或較便宜的前後順序是否正確。

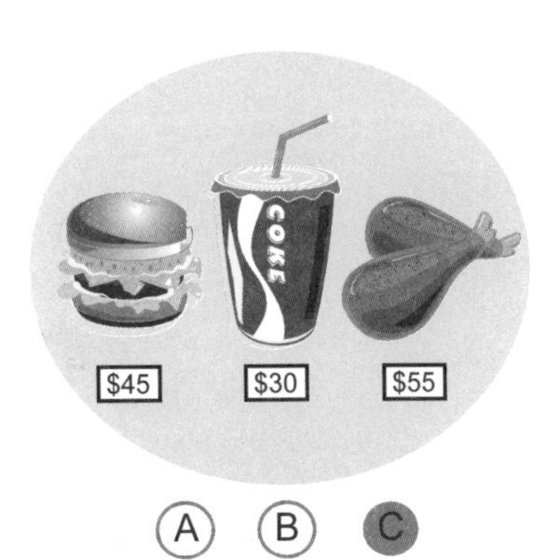

Ⓐ Ⓑ Ⓒ

Q: How much does the fried chicken cost?

(A) It costs forty-five dollars.

(B) It costs thirty dollars.

(C) It costs fifty-five dollars.

問題：炸雞要花多少錢？

(A) 要花四十五元。

(B) 要花三十元。

(C) 要花五十五元。

學習重點

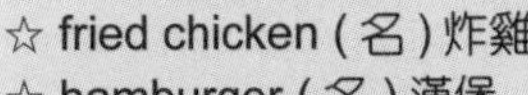

☆ fried chicken (名) 炸雞
☆ hamburger (名) 漢堡
☆ coke (名) 可樂
比較 cock (名) 公雞

Q: What is true about the shoes and the T-shirt?

(A) The T-shirt is more expensive than the shoes.

(B) The T-shirt is cheaper than the shoes.

(C) The T-shirt is the same price as the shoes.

問題：有關鞋子和T恤，何者為真？

(A) T恤比鞋子貴。

(B) T恤比鞋子便宜。

(C) T恤和鞋子價格相同。

學習重點

☆ expensive (形) 昂貴的
☆ cheaper (形) 較便宜的
(cheap 的比較級)

Let's Practice! 聽力練習

Q1

Q2

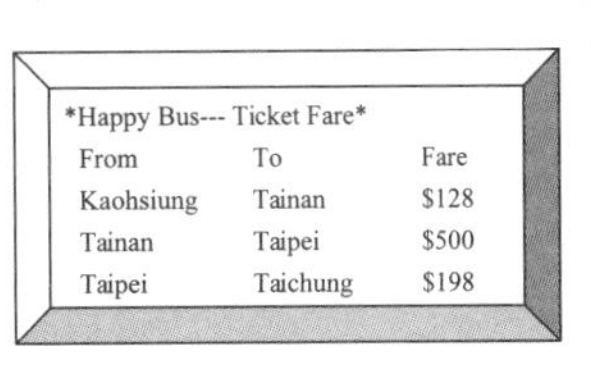

Happy Bus--- Ticket Fare

From	To	Fare
Kaohsiung	Tainan	$128
Tainan	Taipei	$500
Taipei	Taichung	$198

TIPS:

MP3：L07-part1-7

問位置與地點的題型，最常用到的就是表示地點的各種介系詞 in / on / at、或是介系詞片語 in front of / between…and / next to 等等，平常多加練習這些介系詞與片語的使用，聽到 Where 開頭的問句就不用緊張了。

Ⓐ Ⓑ Ⓒ

Q: Where are the children?

(A) They are playing basketball.

(B) They are my sister and brother.

(C) They are on the train.

問題：孩子們在哪裡？

(A) 他們正在打籃球。

(B) 他們是我妹妹和弟弟。

(C) 他們在火車上。

☆ on the train (片語) 在火車上

☆ basketball (名) 籃球

Ⓐ Ⓑ Ⓒ

Q: Where is the school?

(A) It's in back of the MRT Station.

(B) It's on Main Street.

(C) It's next to Jay's home.

問題：學校在哪裡？

(A) 它在捷運車站的後面。

(B) 它在主街上。

(C) 它在杰家的隔壁。

☆ in back of (片語) 在…的後方

☆ next to (片語) 在隔壁

Let's Practice! 聽力練習

Q1

Q2

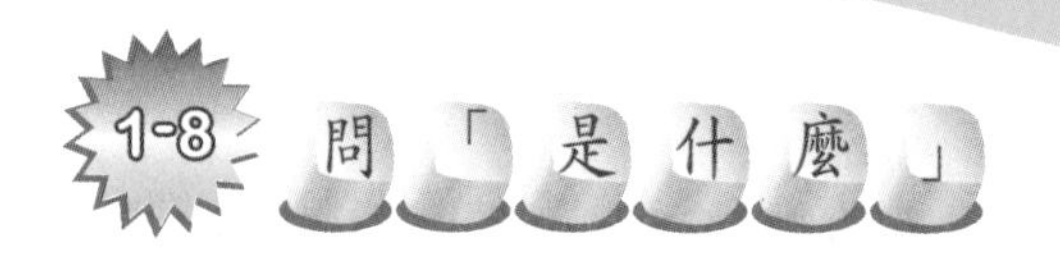

TIPS:

MP3：L08-part1-8

這類題型常會問應試者看到什麼東西，要小心沒有出現在圖片中的選項，若是圖片有出現的事物，則要注意數目或位置是否正確。

Ⓐ Ⓑ Ⓒ

Q: What can we see in this picture?

(A) birds

(B) mountains

(C) people

問題：我們可以在圖片中看到什麼？

(A) 鳥。

(B) 山。

(C) 人們。

☆ see (動) 看見

☆ mountain (名) 山

Ⓐ Ⓑ Ⓒ

Q: What do you see in the picture?

(A) There are three people sitting on the mat.

(B) There is a boy sitting in the tree.

(C) They're having hamburgers.

問題：你在圖中看到什麼？

(A) 有三個人坐在地墊上。

(B) 有一個男孩坐在樹上。

(C) 他們正在吃漢堡。

☆ in the tree (片語) 在樹上

☆ mat (名) 地墊

Let's Practice! 聽力練習

Q1

Q2

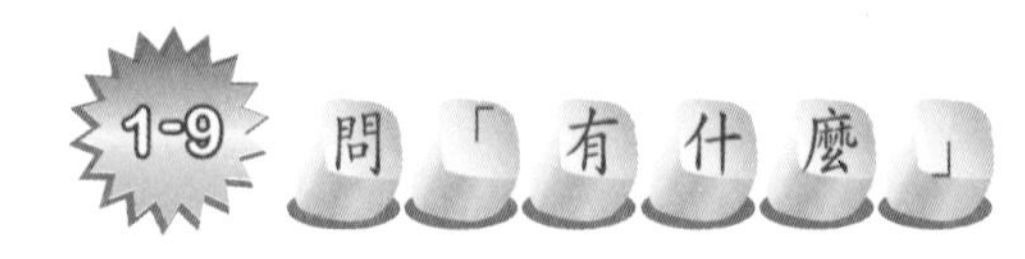

MP3： L09-part1-9

TIPS:
問「有什麼」的題型，要注意是否有其它物品同時出現在圖片中，並聽清楚題目問的東西是什麼。

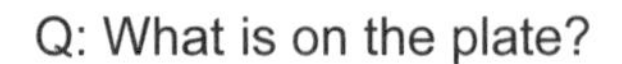

Q: What is on the plate?

(A) tofu

(B) steak

(C) pudding

問題：盤子上有什麼？

(A) 豆腐。

(B) 牛排。

(C) 布丁。

Ⓐ  

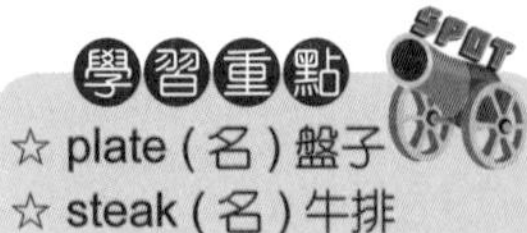

☆ plate（名）盤子
☆ steak（名）牛排
☆ pudding（名）布丁

Q: What is the woman holding in her hand?

(A) A knife.

(B) An iron.

(C) A calculator.

問題：這個女生手上拿著什麼？

(A) 一把刀。

(B) 一支熨斗。

(C) 一台計算機。

Ⓐ Ⓑ Ⓒ

☆ knife（名）刀子
☆ iron（名）熨斗；鐵
（動）熨燙（衣物）
☆ calculator（名）計算機

Let's Practice! 聽力練習

Q1

Ⓐ Ⓑ Ⓒ

Q2

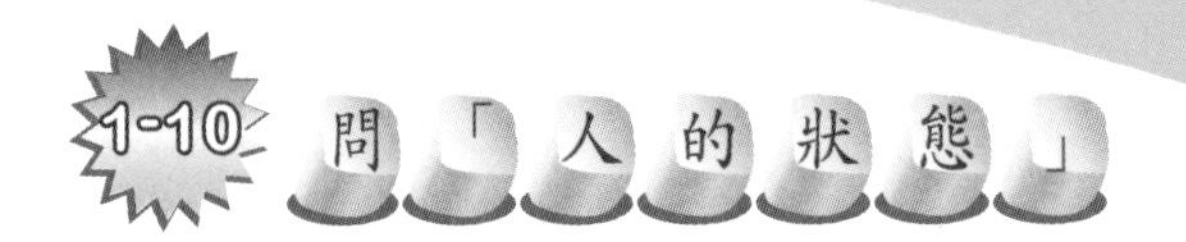

1-10 問「人的狀態」

TIPS: MP3：L10-part1-10

狀態理解是看圖辨義考題裡難度較高的題型，因為問句不像問地點通常用 Where，問價格通常用 How much。在這類題型中，像是 Why(為什麼)、或是問方法的 How(如何…)也很常出現，尤其是人的狀態，像是搭車、通行的方式、或是某人處於某種狀態等等，聽題時要小心。

Q: Why is the man running?

(A) He loves running.

(B) He can't catch the bus.

(C) He is crazy.

問題：為什麼那男人在跑？

(A) 他喜歡跑步。

(B) 他趕不上公車。

(C) 他瘋了。

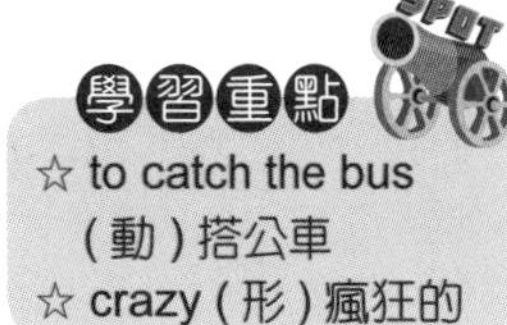

學習重點

☆ to catch the bus (動) 搭公車

☆ crazy (形) 瘋狂的

Q: How do they go to work?

(A) They go to work by bus.

(B) They go to work by bicycle.

(C) They go to work by motorcycle.

問題：他們如何上班？

(A) 他們搭公車上班。

(B) 他們騎腳踏車上班。

(C) 他們騎機車上班。

學習重點

☆ motorcycle (名) 機車

☆ bicycle (名) 腳踏車

Let's Practice! 聽力練習

Q1

Q2

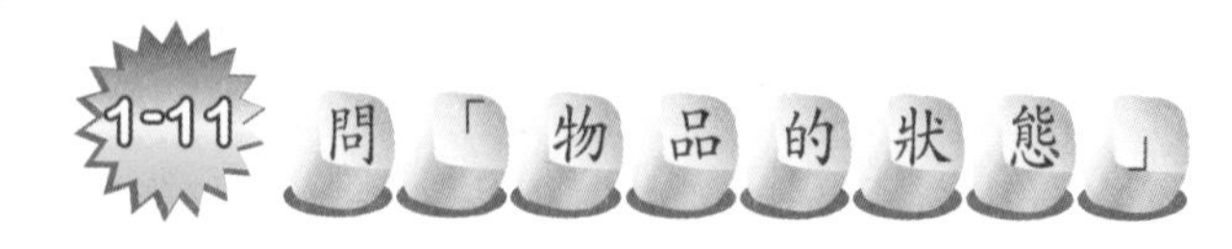

1-11 問「物品的狀態」

TIPS: MP3：L11-part1-11

問物品狀態的題型，主要都是問物品的外觀或樣式，答題時聽清楚選項大多都能輕易拿分。

Ⓐ Ⓑ Ⓒ

Q: What can we say about the coffee?

(A) It is hot.

(B) It is sweet.

(C) It is cold.

問題：我們能說這杯咖啡如何？

(A) 它是熱的。

(B) 它是甜的。

(C) 它是冷的。

Ⓐ Ⓑ Ⓒ

Q: What can we say about the beer?

(A) It's hot.

(B) It's icy.

(C) It's yummy.

問題：我們能說啤酒如何？

(A) 它是熱的。

(B) 它是冰的。

(C) 它很美味。

Let's Practice! 聽力練習

Q1

Q2

Ⓐ Ⓑ Ⓒ

1-12 問「人的外表」

TIPS:　　　　MP3：L12-part1-12

看圖辨義題目中有許多題目都和人有關，若是描述外表，通常和穿的服裝或頭髮長短有關，比較容易混淆的是二或三個人排列在一起，這時要注意圖中人的名字或排列的順序，以免誤解題意。

Ⓐ Ⓑ Ⓒ

Q: What do we know about the girl?

(A) She feels angry.

(B) She wears a dress.

(C) She hates flowers.

問題：關於這個女孩我們知道什麼？

(A) 她覺得生氣。

(B) 她穿洋裝。

(C) 她討厭花。

☆ feel (動) 感覺
☆ dress (名) 洋裝

Q: What is the second person in line wearing?

(A) A skirt.

(B) A suit.

(C) A cap.

問題：第二個人穿著什麼？

(A) 一件裙子。

(B) 一套西裝。

(C) 一頂帽子。

Ⓐ Ⓑ Ⓒ

☆ skirt (名) 裙子
☆ suit (名) 西裝
☆ cap (名) 便帽
比較 hat (名) 寬邊帽

Let's Practice! 聽力練習

Q1

Ⓐ Ⓑ Ⓒ

Q2

1-13 問「人的情緒」

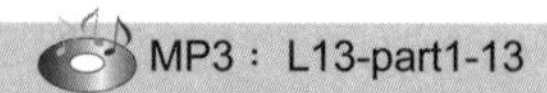

TIPS:
關於人的情緒描述，只要聽清楚題目的選項，就可以輕易拿分。

MP3：L13-part1-13

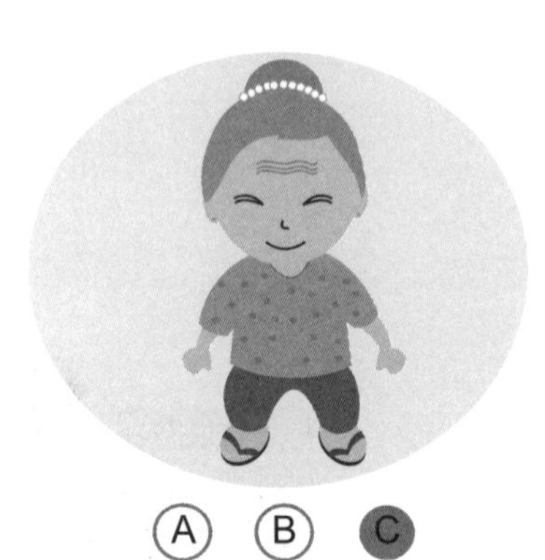

Ⓐ Ⓑ Ⓒ

Q: What can we say about the old woman?

(A) She is mad.

(B) She is tired.

(C) She is happy.

問題：我們可以說這位老太太如何？

(A) 她很生氣。

(B) 她很疲倦。

(C) 她很開心。

學習重點
☆ mad (形) 生氣的
☆ tired (形) 疲倦的

Ⓐ Ⓑ Ⓒ

Q: How does the man feel?

(A) He feels angry.

(B) He feels happy.

(C) He feels sad.

問題：這個男人覺得如何？

(A) 他覺得生氣。

(B) 他覺得開心。

(C) 他覺得難過。

學習重點
☆ angry (形) 生氣的
比較 hungry(形) 饑餓的
☆ sad (形) 難過的；悲傷的

Let's Practice! 聽力練習

Q1

Ⓐ Ⓑ Ⓒ

Q2

Ⓐ Ⓑ Ⓒ

1-14 問「人的嗜好」

MP3：L14-part1-14

TIPS:
描述人的嗜好時，只要聽清楚選項中的內容，熟悉運動或休閒項目的英文單字，要拿分其實很容易。

Ⓐ Ⓑ Ⓒ

Q: What can the girl do?

(A) She can play the violin.

(B) She can play baseball.

(C) She can speak English.

問題：這位女孩會什麼？

(A) 她會拉小提琴。

(B) 她會打棒球。

(C) 她會說英文。

學習重點
☆ violin (名) 小提琴
☆ baseball (名) 棒球

Ⓐ Ⓑ Ⓒ

Q: What is the woman's hobby?

(A) Seeing a movie.

(B) Riding a horse.

(C) Playing tennis.

問題：這個女生的嗜好是什麼？

(A) 看電影。

(B) 騎馬。

(C) 打網球。

學習重點
☆ hobby (名) 嗜好
☆ ride (動) 騎乘
☆ tennis (名) 網球

Let's Practice! 聽力練習

Q1

Ⓐ Ⓑ Ⓒ

Q2

Ⓐ Ⓑ Ⓒ

TIPS:

MP3：L15-part1-15

問人職業的題型，聽題時要注意題目是「What is 人？」或「What do/does 人 do?」，不要與「What is 人 doing?」或「How do/does 人 do?」混淆了。

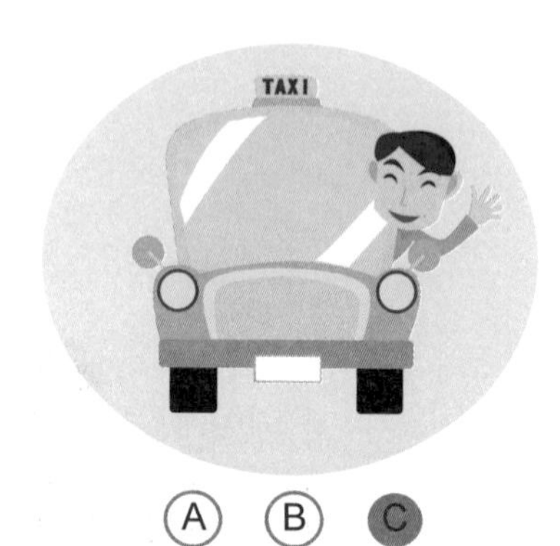

Ⓐ Ⓑ Ⓒ

Q: What is the man?

(A) He is a father.

(B) He is a director.

(C) He is a taxi driver.

問題：這個男人是做什麼的？

(A) 他是一位父親。

(B) 他是一名導演。

(C) 他是一位計程車司機。

☆ taxi driver (名) 計程車司機
☆ director (名) 導演

Ⓐ Ⓑ Ⓒ

Q: What does the man do?

(A) He's a policeman.

(B) He's a fireman.

(C) He's a bartender.

問題：這個男人是做什麼的？

(A) 他是一位警察。

(B) 他是一位消防員。

(C) 他是一位調酒師。

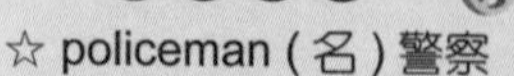
☆ policeman (名) 警察
☆ fireman (名) 消防員
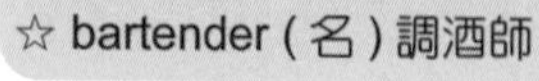
☆ bartender (名) 調酒師

Let's Practice! 聽力練習

Q1

Ⓐ Ⓑ Ⓒ

Q2

Ⓐ  Ⓑ  Ⓒ

1-16 問「正在做什麼」

MP3：L16-part1-16

TIPS:
這類題型最容易與之前提到的「問職業」題型混淆，如果是問「某人正在做什麼」，聽的時候要注意問句結尾是否有加 -ing 或 doing。

Q: What is the man doing?

(A) He is eating.

(B) He is painting.

(C) He is watching TV.

問題：這個男生正在做什麼？

(A) 他正在吃東西。

(B) 他正在畫圖。

(C) 他正在看電視。

Q; What is the girl looking at?

(A) She is crying.

(B) Her skirt is red.

(C) She is looking at ants.

問題：那女孩在看什麼？

(A) 她正在哭。

(B) 她的裙子是紅色的。

(C) 她正在看螞蟻。

Ⓐ Ⓑ Ⓒ

Let's Practice! 聽力練習

Q1

Q2

1-17 問「將要做什麼」

TIPS:

MP3：L17-part1-17

這類題型最容易與「be 動詞 + doing」的句子混淆，聽題時要注意問句中是 (be) going to 還是 (be) doing，並注意選項中的內容，要拿分其實不難。

Ⓐ Ⓑ Ⓒ

Q: What is the man going to do?

(A) go to bed

(B) play basketball

(C) take a trip

問題：這個男生將要做什麼？

(A) 上床睡覺。

(B) 打籃球。

(C) 去旅遊。

學習重點

☆ to take a trip（片語）去旅遊

Ⓐ Ⓑ Ⓒ

Q: What is the boy going to do?

(A) He's going to sleep.

(B) He's going to have breakfast.

(C) He's going to play baseball.

問題：這個男孩要做什麼？

(A) 他要去睡覺。

(B) 他要去吃早餐。

(C) 他要去打棒球。

學習重點

☆ sleep（動）睡覺

☆ breakfast（名）早餐

☆ to play baseball（片語）打棒球

Let's Practice! 聽力練習

Q1

Ⓐ Ⓑ Ⓒ

Q2

Ⓐ Ⓑ Ⓒ

1-18 問「何者為真」

MP3： L18-part1-18

TIPS:
True 或 Not true 的題型難度較高，要先看清楚圖片中的內容、人物所在的地點或進行的動件，然後集中精神聽選項所敘述的內容，才能找到正確的答案。

Q: What is TRUE about the man?

(A) He's studying.

(B) He's playing golf.

(C) He's cooking in the kitchen.

問題：關於這個男人何者為真？

(A) 他正在用功讀書。

(B) 他正在打高爾夫球。

(C) 他正在廚房煮東西。

Ⓐ Ⓑ Ⓒ

學習重點

☆ study (動) 用功讀書
☆ kitchen (名) 廚房

Q: What is TRUE about the woman?

(A) She has long black hair.

(B) She's wearing a dress.

(C) There is a bunch of flowers in her hand.

問題：關於這個女生何者為真？

(A) 她有一頭黑色的長髮。

(B) 她穿著一件洋裝。

(C) 在她手中有一束花。

Ⓐ Ⓑ Ⓒ

學習重點

☆ bunch (名) (一) 束

Let's Practice! 聽力練習

Q1

Ⓐ  

Q2

TIPS:

MP3：L19-part1-19

問「何者不是真的」的題型，比上述問「何者為真」的題型難度更高，因此聽的時候要注意題目敘述的是要問 True 還是 Not true，以免答題時被誤導。

Ⓐ Ⓑ Ⓒ

Q: What is NOT true about the picture?

(A) She's listening to the radio.

(B) She's reading a book.

(C) She's taking a walk.

問題：關於這張圖何者不是真的？

(A) 她正在聽收音機。

(B) 她正在讀一本書。

(C) 她正在散步。

☆ to listen to the radio（片語）聽廣播

☆ to take a walk（片語）散步

Q: What is NOT true about the man?

(A) He is a vendor.

(B) He is selling the clothes.

(C) He is a policeman.

(A) 他是一個小販。

(B) 他正在賣衣服。

(C) 他是一位警察。

☆ vendor（名）小販

☆ sell（動）販賣

☆ policeman（名）警察

Let's Practice! 聽力練習

Q1

Q2

YOUR TURN! 實力挑戰題 MP3： L20-part1- 實力挑戰題

GEPT 初級聽力 Starter

第二部份 問答

問答題型通常是一句招呼、驚嘆、單純的敘述或是疑問句。不同的情境會有不同的回答方式。記得答題前可以先看選項內容再聽題，有助於更快速找到正確答案哦！

範例題： Do you come from Taiwan?

(A) Yes, I will come.

(B) No, I come to America.

(C) Yes, I do.

正確答案為 (C)

TIPS:

MP3： L21-part2-1

招呼類的句型在口語表達中常用得到，但在書寫英文裡不見得看得到，像 See you later.(等會見)、Long time no see.(好久不見)等，要熟練日常生活中與鄰居或親友碰面時打招呼的句型才容易拿分！

A) Thank you.

B) Here you are.

C) Nice to meet you.

Q: Hi, I'm your new classmate.

問題：嗨，我是你的新同學。

(A) 謝謝。

(B) 給你。

(C) 很高興認識你。

☆ Nice to meet you.
= It's nice to meet you.
也可以說 Glad to meet you.

A) I didn't go to the movies last night.

B) Pretty good. How about you?

C) I bought a new dress yesterday.

Q: Long time no see! How have you been?

問題：好久不見！你過得如何？

(A) 我昨晚沒有去看電影。

(B) 很好。你呢？

(C) 我昨天買了一件新洋裝。

☆ Long time no see.
其實是中文「好久不見」錯譯而來的，原本只在華人圈之間使用，之後漸漸進入英文之中，成為口語中常聽得到的見面招呼用語。

A) See you.

B) I can see you.

C) I see the Monday.

Q: See you next Monday.

問題：下星期一見。

(A) 再見。

(B) 我看得見你。

(C) 我看到星期一。

☆ See you.
是口語中「再見」的意思，也可以說 Catch you later.

問答

Let's Practice! 聽力練習

Q1

(A) I am pretty good.

(B) I feel cold.

(C) I am fifteen years old.

Q2

(A) Nothing much.

(B) No news is good news.

(C) The book is new.

2-2 表達讚美與祝福

TIPS:

MP3： L22-part2-2

表達讚美與祝福的題型，回答時通常會用 Thank you.，或是相同的祝福回覆對方，先看清楚選項再聽問題才不容易選錯。

(A) I don't have luck.

(B) Thank you.

(C) You must be lucky.

Q: Good luck!

問題：祝你好運！

(A) 我沒有運氣。

(B) 謝謝。

(C) 你一定很幸運。

學習重點

☆ Good luck.
= I wish you good luck.
☆ luck (名) 運氣
→ good luck 好運
→ bad luck 壞運
☆ lucky (形) 幸運的

(A) Yes, it is.

(B) It's fine.

(C) I am cute.

Q: How cute the baby is!

問題：這個嬰兒多可愛啊！

(A) 是啊，他是。

(B) 它很好。

(C) 我很可愛。

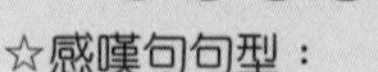

☆感嘆句句型：
How + 形容詞 + 主詞 + be 動詞 + !

(A) I am happy.

(B) Happy New Year to you, too.

(C) Happy birthday!

Q: Happy New Year!

問題：新年快樂！

(A) 我很快樂。

(B) 也祝你新年快樂。

(C) 生日快樂！

比較

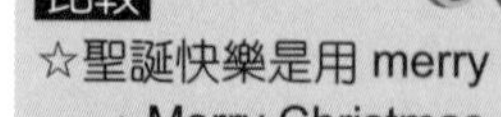

→ Merry Christmas
☆新年快樂是用 happy
→ Happy New Year

Let's Practice! 聽力練習

Q1

(A) Thank you.

(B) That's right.

(C) No, it's hot today.

Q2

(A) Happy birthday.

(B) That's great.

(C) Good luck!

2-3 感謝與致歉

TIPS:　　MP3：L23-part2-3

表示感謝或致歉的問答題型，只要平常多練習相關的回答方式，很容易就可以選出答案。

Q: Thanks for your help!

問題：謝謝你的幫忙！

A) What's wrong with you?

B) I need your help.

C) It's not a big deal.

(A) 你怎麼搞的？

(B) 我需要你的幫忙。

(C) 這沒什麼。

學習重點

☆ It's not a big deal.
[沒什麼，不用客氣。]

☆ need (動) 需要

Q: You did me a great favor. Thank you so much.

問題：你幫了我大忙。真的十分感謝你。

A) Thank you.

B) That's all right.

C) Never mind.

(A) 謝謝。

(B) 沒關係。

(C) 別介意。

學習重點

☆ Never mind. [別介意，不用客氣。]

☆ That's all right. [沒關係]

That's all right. 通常會用在對方表示歉意或無法做到目標時的回答。Never mind. 則有「小事一樁、不用客氣」的意思。

Q: I'm really sorry.

問題：我真的很抱歉。

A) I am, too.

B) It's not your fault.

C) Don't mention it.

(A) 我也是。

(B) 這不是你的錯。

(D) 不必客氣。

學習重點

☆ fault (名) 錯誤

☆ Don't mention it.
[不客氣。]

Let's Practice! 聽力練習

Q1

(A) I'm sorry to hear that.

(B) You're welcome.

(C) That's all right.

Q2

(A) Not at all.

(B) Nice to meet you.

(C) It's kind of you to say so.

2-4 電話用語

TIPS: MP3： L24-part2-4

電話用語一定要記得，回答「我就是」時，要用 This is him/her. 或直接回答 Speaking.，不可以用 I am. 或 I am talking. 來回答。

(A) Maybe.
(B) This is Jack speaking.
(C) Yes, you may.

Q: May I speak to Jack?

問題：我可以跟傑克說話嗎？

(A) 也許。
(B) 我是傑克，請說。
(C) 是的，你可以。

☆ May I…?
[我可以…嗎？]
電話用語中的 May I speak to... 回答時不可用 Yes/No 回答，而是要回答 Speaking(我就是)或是 Hold on(等一下)。

(A) I am.
(B) Speaking.
(C) That's me.

Q: Hello. This is Ruby. Is Lisa there?

問題：哈囉。我是露比。莉莎在嗎？

(A) 我是。
(B) 我就是，請說。
(C) 那是我。

Speaking 意思指「就是我，我正在說」，電話用語裡要用 Speaking，不能用 I am。

(A) This is Jack speaking.
(B) Your mother is calling.
(C) 2707-1669

Q: What number are you calling at?

問題：你打幾號？

(A) 我是傑克。
(B) 你媽媽打電話來。
(C) 2707-1669。

☆ number (名) 號碼；數字
☆ phone number (名) 電話號碼
☆打電話要用 call at + 電話號碼

Let's Practice! 聽力練習

Q1

(A) There is Benson.
(B) Yes, he is there.
(C) Who is speaking?

Q2

(A) I'm sorry. There is no one by that name.
(B) Nice to meet you!
(C) I'm here. May I help you?

2-5 問數量與價格

MP3： L25-part2-5

TIPS:
詢問「數量」的問句中，最常出現的問句就是 How many…？這時答句就要選有確切數量的回答；如果是問「價格」，問句則通常會用 How much…？聽問題時要分清楚才不會選錯答案哦！

A) I have two brothers.
B) I have three balls.
C) I have many brothers.

Q: How many brothers do you have?
問題：你有幾位兄弟？
(A) 我有兩位兄弟。
(B) 我有三顆球。
(C) 我有很多兄弟。

☆ How many…? [有多少]
☆ brother (名) 兄弟

A) It took me three hours.
B) I spent a whole day.
C) I spent two thousand dollars.

Q: How much did you spend on the purse?
問題：這個錢包你花了多少錢？
(A) 它花了我三小時。
(B) 我花了一整天。
(C) 我花了兩千元。

☆ How much + do/does + 人 + spend…? […花了多少錢？]

A) They are cheap.
B) It is three hundred.
C) They are two hundred.

Q: How much is the skirt?
問題：這條裙子多少錢？
(A) 它們很便宜。
(B) 它要三百。
(C) 它們要兩百。

☆ How much…? […多少錢？]
☆ cheap (形) 便宜的

Let's Practice! 聽力練習

Q1
(A) Two.
(B) I have a girlfriend.
(C) My mom has two sisters.

Q2
(A) Two hours.
(B) Last week.
(C) Five hundred NT dollars.

2-6 問次數

MP3：L26-part2-6

TIPS:
問次數的問句大多為「How often…？」聽到問句為 How often 時，就可以大膽選擇表示活動次數或動作頻率的答案。

(A) I often play bowling.
(B) Playing bowling is fun.
(C) Once a week.

Q: How often do you play bowling?
問題：你多久打一次保齡球？
(A) 我常打保齡球。
(B) 打保齡球很好玩。
(C) 一週一次。

☆ How often…?
[多久…(一次)?]
☆ bowling (名) 保齡球

(A) With his mom.
(B) Once a week.
(C) On Sunday.

Q: How often does George go surfing?
問題：喬治多久去衝浪一次？
(A) 和他媽媽。
(B) 一週一次。
(C) 在週日。

☆ surf (動) 衝浪
☆ once (副) 一次

(A) It tastes delicious.
(B) Every day.
(C) It cost them five hundred dollars.

Q: How often do they eat fast food?
問題：他們多久吃一次速食？
(A) 它嚐起來很美味。
(B) 每天。
(C) 它花了他們五百塊錢。

☆ taste (動) 嚐起來
☆ delicious (形) 美味的
☆ cost (動) 花費
☆ fast food (名) 速食

Let's Practice! 聽力練習

Q1

(A) They usually go there.
(B) They often go to the museum.
(C) Once a week.

Q2

(A) Twice a week.
(B) It's at twelve o'clock.
(C) One more time.

MP3：L27-part2-7

TIPS:
問「身份」的句型通常會問到彼此之間的關係，所以一定要熟練人的稱謂與彼此間關係的單字，聽題時才不容易聽錯。

Q: Is she your mother?

問題：她是你媽媽嗎？

A) She is beautiful.
B) Yes, she is.
C) My mother is young.

(A) 她很漂亮。
(B) 是的，她是。
(C) 我媽媽很年輕。

學習重點
☆ beautiful (形) 漂亮的

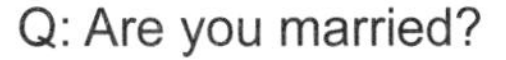

Q: Are you married?

問題：你結婚了嗎？

A) I am merry.
B) Yes, I am.
C) We are angry.

(A) 我很高興。
(B) 是的，我是。
(C) 我們很生氣。

學習重點

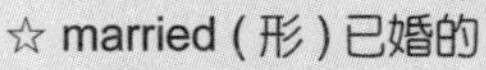

☆ married (形) 已婚的
☆ merry (形) 快樂的
☆ angry (形) 生氣的

Q: Do you know Jason?

問題：你認識傑生嗎？

A) I know Jack.
B) No, I am Ben.
C) Yes, he is my husband.

(A) 我知道傑克。
(B) 不，我是班。
(C) 是的，他是我丈夫。

學習重點
☆ husband (名) 丈夫

Let's Practice! 聽力練習

Q1

(A) She is beautiful.
(B) She is a teacher.
(C) She is nice.

Q2

(A) Yes, I am.
(B) My name is Lily.
(C) How about you?

問答

TIPS:

MP3： L28-part2-8

描述外表時常會用到表示「看起來（如何）」的連綴動詞 look，要注意不要與當一般動詞用的片語 look at 混淆，才不容易選錯答案哦！

(A) She is so attractive.

(B) She is eighteen years old.

(C) She is my sister.

Q: Who is that slim and lovely lady?

問題：那位苗條又可愛的女士是誰啊？

(A) 她很有魅力。

(B) 她十八歲。

(C) 她是我姊姊。

☆ slim（形）苗條的
☆ lovely（形）可愛的
☆ attractive（形）吸引人的；有魅力的

(A) Thank you. I jog every morning.

(B) Yeah, I love this T-shirt.

(C) Don't mention it.

Q: You look fit, David.

問題：大衛，你看起來很健康。

(A) 謝謝。我每天早上都慢跑。

(B) 是啊。我很愛這件 T 恤。

(C) 不用客氣。

☆ fit（形）健康的
☆ jog（動）慢跑
☆ mention（動）提及
☆ Don't mention it. [不用客氣。]

(A) He is fine.

(B) He is 5 feet and 2 inches tall.

(C) He is eight years old.

Q: How tall is your brother?

問題：你弟弟多高？

(A) 他很好。

(B) 他五尺二寸高。

(C) 他八歲。

☆ How tall…? […有多高？]

Let's Practice! 聽力練習

Q1

(A) He is Monica's grandpa.

(B) He is singing.

(C) I met him this morning.

Q2

(A) She is my grandmother.

(B) No, she is young.

(C) She is in the classroom.

2-9 描述情緒與身體狀況

MP3：L29-part2-9

TIPS:
表達情緒或身體狀況時，也常用得到連綴動詞 look(看起來) 和 feel(感覺起來)，回答問題前可以先看答案，聽到問題後就能快速答題。

(A) My puppy is dead.
(B) I'm going to the library.
(C) I will study English.

Q: You look sad. What's going on?
問題：你看起來很傷心。發生什麼事了？

(A) 我的小狗狗死了。
(B) 我要去圖書館。
(C) 我要讀英文了。

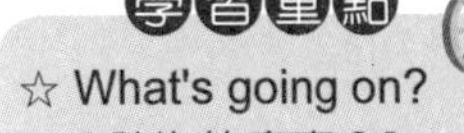
學習重點
☆ What's going on? [發生什麼事？]
☆ dead (形) 死了的
☆ puppy (名) 小狗

(A) Yes, thank you.
(B) That's great.
(C) It tasted good.

Q: Do you feel better now?
問題：你現在有覺得好一點嗎？
(A) 是的，謝謝。
(B) 那很棒。
(C) 它嚐起來不錯。

學習重點
☆ better (形) 較好的 (good 的比較級)

(A) Do you need a tire?
(B) I feel happy.
(C) You had better go to bed early.

Q: I feel tired.
問題：我覺得很累。
(A) 你需要一個輪胎嗎？
(B) 我覺得開心。
(C) 你最好早點上床睡覺。

學習重點

☆ tired (形) 感到疲累的
☆ tire (名) 輪胎
(動) 使~勞累
☆ had better (片語) 最好…

Let's Practice! 聽力練習

Q1

(A) I love to eat toast.
(B) Take it easy. You can make it.
(C) You did a good job.

Q2

(A) Would you like to have some hot tea?
(B) Let's go swimming.
(C) Take off your coat.

TIPS:　MP3：L30-part2-10

表達喜好的題型，常會用到 Which 的問句，或是在直述句後加上要對方附和的附加問句，回答這類題型時要注意，回答內容為肯定時答 Yes，若內容為否定才回答 No。

(A) He feels tired.

(B) Hot dog.

(C) He likes both.

Q: Which does he like, rice or noodles?

問題：他喜歡什麼，米飯還是麵條？

(A) 他覺得很累。

(B) 熱狗。

(C) 他兩個都喜歡。

☆ rice (名) 米飯
☆ noodle (名) 麵條
☆ both (代) 兩者 (皆)

(A) I like action movies.

(B) So do I.

(C) Yes, I like it.

Q: I like cheesecake.

問題：我喜歡起司蛋糕。

(A) 我喜歡動作片。

(B) 我也是。

(C) 是的，我喜歡。

☆ cheesecake (名) 起司蛋糕
☆ action movie (名) 動作片

(A) Isn't it a fish?

(B) Yes, it's really tasty.

(C) No, it is.

Q: It's delicious, isn't it?

問題：它很美味，不是嗎？

(A) 它不是魚嗎？

(B) 是的，它真的很美味。

(C) 不，它是。

☆ delicious (形) 美味的
☆ tasty (形) 美味的

Let's Practice! 聽力練習

Q1

(A) So do I.

(B) Neither do I.

(C) Don't mention it.

Q2

(A) I like fish.

(B) I like zebra.

(C) I like kangaroo.

MP3： L31-part2-11

TIPS:
表達嗜好的句型一定會提到 hobby，這個字的發音和 habit 很接近，聽題目時要小心不要聽錯哦！

(A) I like to collect stamps.
(B) I have good habits.
(C) They are cute.

Q: What are your hobbies?
問題：你的嗜好是什麼？
(A) 我喜歡收集郵票。
(B) 我有好習慣。
(C) 他們很可愛。

☆ hobby (名) 嗜好
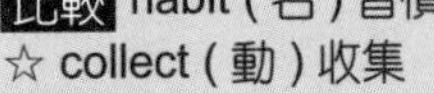
比較 habit (名) 習慣
☆ collect (動) 收集
☆ stamp (名) 郵票

問答

(A) Why not?
(B) Don't mention it!
(C) I practice every day.

Q: How did you play football so well?
問題：你美式足球怎麼踢得這麼好？
(A) 為什麼不？
(B) 別客氣！
(C) 我每天練習。

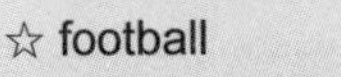

☆ football (名) 美式足球
☆ mention (動) 提及
☆ practice (動) 練習

(A) Yes, I do.
(B) Let's go.
(C) Let's have lunch.

Q: I want to go mountain climbing.
問題：我想去爬山。
(A) 是的，我是。
(B) 我們一起去吧。
(C) 我們一起去吃午餐吧。

☆ to go mountain climbing (片語) 去登山
☆ lunch (名) 午餐

Let's Practice! 聽力練習

Q1

(A) I'm not free tonight.
(B) Twice a week.
(C) See a movie.

Q2

(A) I played basketball with them yesterday.
(B) Let's play basketball.
(C) We practice playing basketball every day.

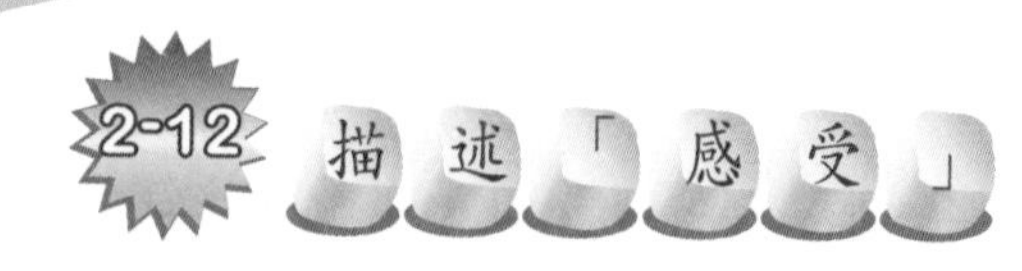

TIPS:
MP3：L32-part2-12
詢問人對某事物或經驗的感受常會用 How is/was…? 或是問 Do you like…? 的句型，答題前先看選項內容再聽題，很快就能找到正確答案。

(A) The party was on Sunday.
(B) We had a good time there.
(C) I enjoy reading books.

Q: Did you enjoy the party last night?
問題：你喜歡昨晚的派對嗎？
(A) 派對是在星期天。
(B) 我們玩得很開心。
(C) 我喜歡看書。

☆ enjoy（動）享受；喜愛
☆ to have a good time（片語）玩得開心

(A) We went to the circus.
(B) It will begin in ten minutes.
(C) It's really interesting.

Q: What do you think of the show?
問題：你覺得那個表演如何？
(A) 我們去看馬戲表演。
(B) 它十分鐘之內會開始。
(C) 它很有趣。

☆ to think of（片語）認為，覺得
☆ interesting（形）有趣的
☆ circus（名）馬戲團
☆ begin（動）開始

(A) Yes, I like it.
(B) I like singing.
(C) I do like eating kiwi.

Q: Do you like Hello Kitty?
問題：你喜歡凱蒂貓嗎？
(A) 是的，我喜歡它。
(B) 我喜歡唱歌。
(C) 我真的很喜歡吃奇異果。

☆ Hello Kitty（名）凱蒂貓
☆ kiwi（名）奇異果
☆ do + 原形動詞 [真的（做了）…]

Let's Practice! 聽力練習

Q1

(A) It's yummy.
(B) I saw the movie with Peter yesterday.
(C) It's so touching.

Q2

(A) That's too bad.
(B) From December 20th to January 5th.
(C) Great! I took a trip to Italy.

2-13 問「正在做什麼」

TIPS: MP3：L33-part2-13

表示「正在做某事」的題型，常會出現主詞單複數不同的選項混淆答題者，或是同為現在進行式的選項，但所做的動作和問題裡敘述的不同，聽題時要完整聽完動作為何，才不容易答錯。

A) We're playing cards.
B) They're practicing skating.
C) He is taking a bath.

Q: What are you doing?
問題：你們在做什麼？
(A) 我們在玩牌。
(B) 他們在練習溜冰。
(C) 他正在洗澡。

☆ to play cards (片語) 玩牌
☆ skate (動) 溜冰
☆ to take a bath (片語) 洗澡

A) Yes, there is a TV show.
B) I'm taking a shower, too.
C) No, she's sleeping in her room.

Q: Is Nancy taking a shower in the bathroom?
問題：南西正在浴室沖澡嗎？
(A) 是的，有一個電視節目。
(B) 我也在沖澡。
(C) 不，她在她房間裡睡覺。

☆ to take a shower (片語) 淋浴
☆ sleep (動) 睡覺

(A) Yes, they are waiting for Ruby.
(B) Yes, they are drinking coffee at home.
(C) They are talking on the phone.

Q: Are they still talking in the coffee shop?
問題：他們還在咖啡店裡聊天嗎？
(A) 是的，他們正在等露比。
(B) 是的，他們正在家裡喝咖啡。
(C) 他們正在講電話。

☆ still (副) 仍然
☆ coffee shop (名) 咖啡店
☆ to talk on the phone (片語) 講電話

Let's Practice! 聽力練習

Q1

(A) No, they are playing baseball outside.
(B) Yes, they're sleeping.
(C) No, I'm reading books.

Q2

(A) No, he went to school five minutes ago.
(B) Yes, he's still sleeping at home.
(C) He had a sandwich.

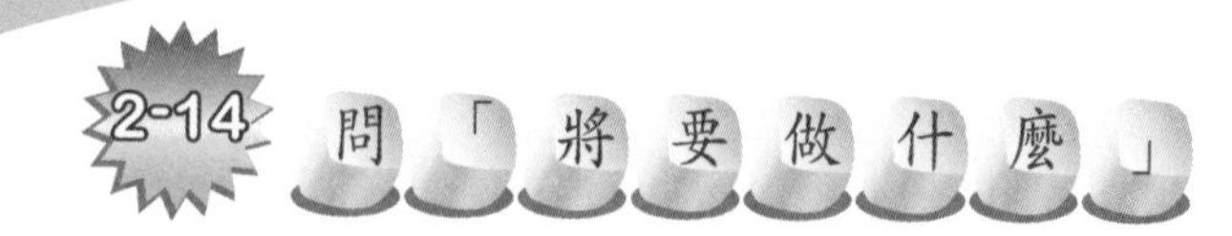

TIPS: MP3：L34-part2-14

這類題型最常出現過去式、現在式和未來式混合的選項，聽題時要注意助動詞是否有 will 或有 be going to 的句型，並聽清楚主詞的人稱為何，才不會掉入選項的陷阱裡。

(A) I was playing video games.
(B) We are going to hold a party.
(C) We are cleaning the house.

Q: What will you do tomorrow?
問題：你明天要做什麼？
(A) 我（當時）正在玩電動。
(B) 我們要舉辦一場派對。
(C) 我們正在打掃房子。

☆ to hold a party（片語）舉辦派對
☆ video game（名）電動玩具
☆ clean（動）打掃（形）乾淨的

(A) Yes, she will.
(B) No, they don't.
(C) Yes, they will.

Q: Will Gina and Nina go to work tomorrow?
問題：吉娜和妮娜明天會去上班嗎？
(A) 是的，她會。
(B) 不，他們沒有。
(C) 是的，他們會。

☆ to go to work（片語）去上班

(A) It depends.
(B) On Park Road.
(C) Come here.

Q: Will you come to my house tomorrow?
問題：你明天會來我家嗎？
(A) 要看情況。
(B) 在公園路。
(C) 過來。

☆ depend（動）依靠
☆ It depends.［要看情況］

Let's Practice! 聽力練習

Q1

(A) I'm still thinking about it.
(B) I went to the party.
(C) How nice it is!

Q2

(A) No, I'll go jogging.
(B) Yes, I'll go to the supermarket.
(C) Yes, I need to go.

2-15 問「過去做了什麼」

MP3： L35-part2-15

TIPS:
問「過去做了某事」的題型中，常會出現選項的主詞與題目所問的不同，聽題時要特別注意所問的主詞為何才不容易選錯。

(A) We took a trip to Singapore.
(B) They were playing Wii.
(C) They read books.

Q: What were they doing at that time?
問題：他們那時正在做什麼？
(A) 我們去新加坡旅遊。
(B) 他們正在玩 Wii。
(C) 他們讀書。

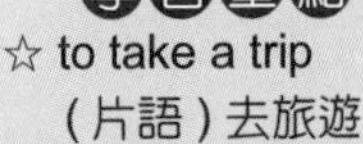
☆ to take a trip (片語) 去旅遊
☆ Singapore (名) 新加坡

(A) I will do it later.
(B) No, I forgot to do it.
(C) No, I did.

Q: You didn't do the homework, did you?
問題：你沒有做你的回家功課，不是嗎？
(A) 我等一下會做。
(B) 沒有，我忘了做。
(C) 不，我做了。

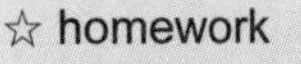
☆ homework (名) 回家功課
☆ later (副) 稍晚
☆ forget (動) 忘記

(A) No, that was a great concert.
(B) I like to go to the concert.
(C) Yes. How did you know?

Q: Did you go to the concert last night?
問題：你有去昨晚的演唱會嗎？
(A) 不，那是場很棒的演唱會。
(B) 我喜歡去演唱會。
(C) 是，你怎麼知道的？

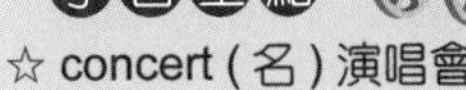
☆ concert (名) 演唱會

Let's Practice! 聽力練習

Q1

(A) How is the movie?
(B) What can I do for you?
(C) Did you enjoy it?

Q2

(A) I'm talking on the phone.
(B) Yes, why didn't you come to school today?
(C) I don't have a cell phone.

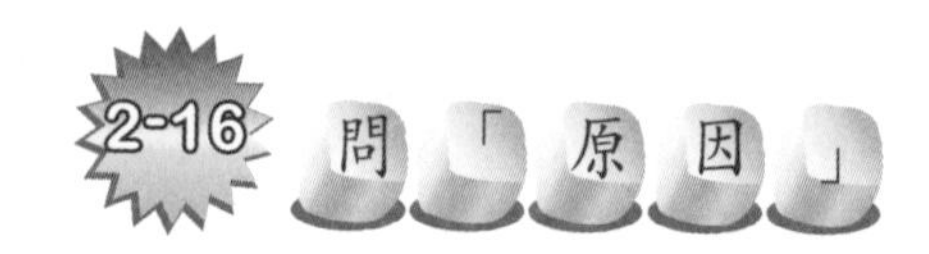

TIPS:

MP3：L36-part2-16

這類題型最常出現的問句就是 Why…? 或 How come?，聽到這類題目，選擇表示原因的句子就對了。

(A) I am late.
(B) I missed the bus.
(C) I miss my grandpa.

Q: Why are you late?
問題：你為什麼遲到？
(A) 我遲到了。
(B) 我錯過公車了。
(C) 我想念我的外公。

☆ late (形) 晚的、遲的
☆ miss (動)
(1) 錯過；(2) 想念

(A) I'm right.
(B) I didn't sleep well last night.
(C) You're wrong.

Q: What's wrong with you?
問題：你哪裡不對勁嗎？
(A) 我是對的。
(B) 我昨晚沒睡好。
(C) 你是錯的。

☆ wrong (形) 錯的；有問題的
☆ right (形) 對的；正確的；右邊的

(A) I will come.
(B) I stayed up late last night.
(C) By bus.

Q: You look so tired. How come?
問題：你看起來很疲累。怎麼了？
(A) 我會來。
(B) 我昨晚熬夜。
(C) 搭公車。

☆ How come?
怎麼會？為何？
☆ to stay up (片語) 熬夜

Let's Practice! 聽力練習

Q1

(A) I went to school by bus.
(B) I got a stomachache.
(C) I have no idea.

Q2

(A) Have a good time!
(B) Thank you for coming.
(C) I decided to lose weight.

TIPS:
表示邀約的問句，主要有三種：(1) Would you like⋯? (2) How about⋯? (3) Let's⋯! 回答時也要注意接受或拒絕的內容是否和題目所問的事物相同。

(A) No, thanks. I'm full.
(B) Yes, I would like a glass of wine.
(C) I like pasta.

Q: Would you like some desserts?
問題：你想要來些甜點嗎？
(A) 不，謝了。我很飽。
(B) 是的，我想要來一杯酒。
(C) 我喜歡義大利麵。

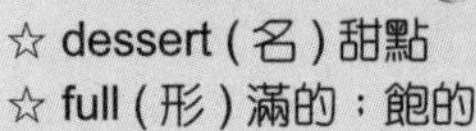

☆ dessert (名) 甜點
☆ full (形) 滿的；飽的
比較 fool (名) 笨蛋

(A) I have a new bike.
(B) Do you want to buy a new one?
(C) That's a great idea.

Q: How about riding the bikes with us?
問題：要不要和我們一起去騎腳踏車？
(A) 我有一輛新腳踏車。
(B) 你要買一輛新的嗎？
(C) 那是個很棒的主意。

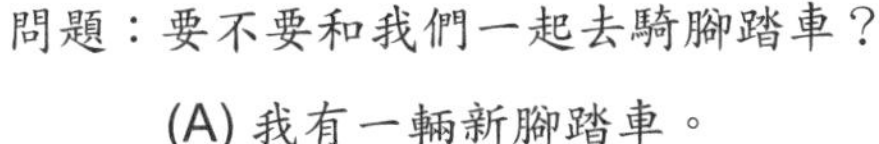

☆ to ride a bike
(片語) 騎腳踏車

(A) Sorry, I have to study English.
(B) Let's stay at home!
(C) It's at the corner.

Q: Let's go to the zoo!
問題：我們一起去動物園吧！
(A) 抱歉，我得去讀英文。
(B) 我們一起待在家裡吧！
(C) 它在轉角。

☆ Let's⋯!
[我們一起⋯吧！]
☆ at the corner
(片語) 在轉角

Let's Practice! 聽力練習

Q1

(A) It's hot today.
(B) Yes, please.
(C) I love beef.

Q2

(A) No, thanks. I'm full.
(B) That's all right.
(C) I don't have the time.

TIPS:

MP3：L38-part2-18

尋求幫助的問答句常會用到片語「give 人 a hand（幫某人的忙）」，要小心不要與「give 人 a big hand（給某人掌聲鼓勵）」混淆了。

Q: Could you please give me a hand?

問題：你可以幫我忙嗎？

(A) Yes, I can give you my hands.

(B) Which hand do you want?

(C) My pleasure.

(A) 是的，我可以給你我的手。

(B) 你想要哪一隻手？

(C) 我的榮幸。

☆ to give 人 a hand（片語）幫忙某人

☆ My pleasure. 我的榮幸

Q: Do you have any suggestions?

問題：你有什麼建議嗎？

(A) I have no idea.

(B) What a good idea it is!

(C) It sounds nice.

(A) 我不知道。

(B) 這是個多麼棒的點子啊！

(C) 聽起來很好。

☆ have no idea（片語）不知道

☆ suggestion（名）建議

Q: Is something bothering you?

問題：有事情困擾你嗎？

(A) I'm sorry to hear that.

(B) I have three brothers.

(C) I don't want to talk about it now!

(A) 我很遺憾聽到這件事。

(B) 我有三個兄弟。

(C) 我現在不想談這個！

☆ bother（動）困擾、干擾

比較 brother（名）兄弟

Let's Practice! 聽力練習

Q1

(A) I have a good idea.

(B) Would you like to drink some water?

(C) No problem.

Q2

(A) Sure. What can I do?

(B) I will help you tomorrow.

(C) I can speak English well.

2-19 詢問「是否可以」

TIPS: MP3：L39-part2-19

詢問「可不可以…？」最重要的句型就是 Can I…? 及 May I…?

注意：這類問題的 May I…？回答通常不會直接答 Yes 或 No，常會用 Sure 或 No problem 來回答。

Q: Mom, can I go out with friends tonight?

問題：媽，我今晚可以和朋友一起出去嗎？

(A) No way!

(B) Let's have dinner.

(C) It's a great night.

(A) 不可以！

(B) 我們一起吃晚餐吧。

(C) 這是個很棒的夜晚。

☆ No way. [不可以]

Q: Do you mind turning off the light?

問題：你介意把燈關上嗎？

(A) It's OK with me.

(B) Turn it down.

(C) Don't mention it!

(A) 我可以，我不介意。

(B) 轉小聲點。

(C) 不用客氣！

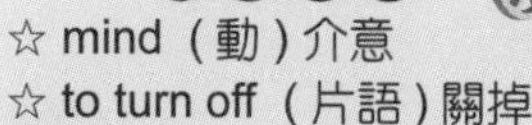

☆ mind（動）介意

☆ to turn off（片語）關掉

比較 to turn on（片語）開啓

Q: May I use your toilet?

問題：我可以借用一下你的洗手間嗎？

(A) What are you talking about?

(B) Make yourself at home.

(C) Take care!

(A) 你在說什麼？

(B) 請便。

(C) 保重！

☆ toilet（名）廁所

☆ Make yourself at home. [請便]

Make yourself at home. 原意是指「把這當你自己家」，也就是「請隨意、請便」的意思。

☆ Take care. [保重]

Let's Practice! 聽力練習

Q1

(A) Of course not.

(B) I have no idea.

(C) This is mine.

Q2

(A) Don't worry.

(B) Sure. Here you are.

(C) I see.

2-20 表達位置

TIPS: MP3：L40-part2-20
詢問位置或地點的題型大部分都會用到 Where 開頭的問句，回答時要用事物所在的位置表達；如果是問路的句型，通常會用 Can you tell me…? 回答時則要指示對方走的路線及方向。

(A) There is a lot of seafood.
(B) It's at the corner.
(C) By bus.

Q: Where is the convenience store?
問題：便利商店在哪裡？
(A) 有很多海鮮。
(B) 在轉角。
(C) 搭公車。

學習重點
☆ convenience store (名) 便利商店
☆ at the corner (片語) 在…轉角
☆ seafood (名) 海鮮

(A) Yes. Just in back of the school.
(B) Do you need some flowers?
(C) I go there by bus.

Q: Is there a grocery store near our school?
問題：我們學校附近有雜貨店嗎？
(A) 有。就在學校的後面。
(B) 你需要一些花嗎？
(C) 我搭公車去那裡。

學習重點
☆ grocery store (名) 雜貨店
☆ in back of (片語) 在…後方

(A) Just walk straight, and turn right.
(B) I often go there to take exercise on Sunday.
(C) You can get there by MRT or by bus.

Q: Could you tell me where the gym is?
問題：可以告訴我健身房在哪裡嗎？
(A) 直走，然後右轉。
(B) 我通常週日去那裡運動。
(C) 你可以搭捷運或搭公車去那裡。

學習重點
☆ gym (名) 健身房
☆ straight (副) 直直地
☆ to take exercise (片語) 做運動

Let's Practice! 聽力練習

Q1

(A) You can go there by bus 212.
(B) Just walk straight, and turn left.
(C) It's two hundred meters.

Q2

(A) It's in the sky.
(B) It's at the corner.
(C) You can take the bus.

2-21 詢問交通方式與距離

TIPS:

MP3：L41-part2-21

How can I…? 或 How do you…? 的問句通常是問「方法」。在問交通方式的題型中，就是要問抵達目的地的方式，所以不能選擇回答與其它地點之間遠近的選項，而是要回答搭乘何種交通工具。

(A) By MRT.

(B) It's next to the coffee shop.

(C) My house is near the station.

Q: How can I get to the station?

問題：我要如何去車站？

(A) 搭捷運。

(B) 它在咖啡店隔壁。

(C) 我家靠近車站。

學習重點

☆ station (名) 車站

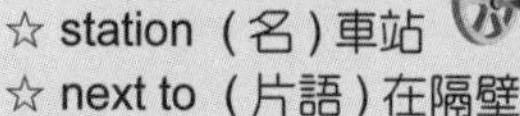

☆ next to (片語) 在隔壁

☆ near (介) 靠近

(A) On the bus.

(B) By train.

(C) Near the Ruby Restaurant.

Q: How do you go to your grandpa's house?

問題：你都是怎麼去你外公家的？

(A) 在公車上。

(B) 搭火車。

(C) 靠近露比餐廳。

學習重點

☆ by + 交通工具 [搭乘 (交通工具)]

☆ on + 交通工具 [在 (交通工具) 上]

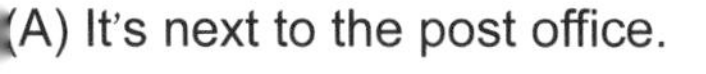

(A) It's next to the post office.

(B) 2 kilometers.

(C) By bus.

Q: How far is it from the beach to your hotel?

問題：你住的飯店離海灘有多遠？

(A) 在郵局隔壁。

(B) 兩公里。

(C) 搭公車。

學習重點

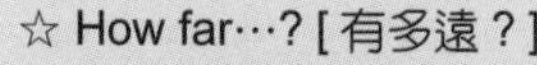

☆ How far…? [有多遠？]

☆ from 甲地 to 乙地 從甲地到乙地

☆ post office (名) 郵局

☆ kilometer (名) 公里

Let's Practice! 聽力練習

Q1

(A) Two hours.

(B) By taxi.

(C) Three million dollars.

Q2

(A) Around 5 miles.

(B) In twenty minutes.

(C) It's close to the station.

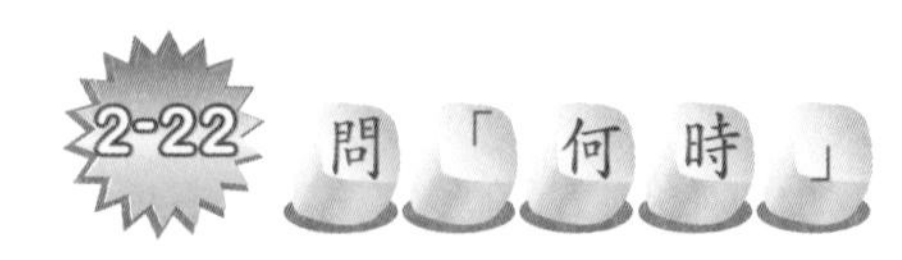

TIPS:

MP3：L42-part2-22

問時間的題目常會以 When 或 What time 開頭，比較容易混淆的是問「星期幾」的「What day」與問「日期」的「What date」，聽問題時要特別小心。

Q: Do you have the time?

問題：你有現在的時間嗎？

(A) I am busy today.
(A) 我今天很忙。

(B) No, I don't have time.
(B) 不，我沒有時間。

(C) Yes, it's ten o'clock.
(C) 有，現在十點。

☆ Do you have the time?
[現在幾點？]

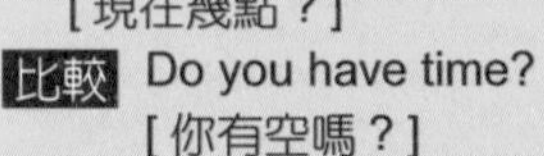

比較 Do you have time?
[你有空嗎？]

問句有the time，意思就是問「(現在 / 手錶上)的時間」，所以答句要選現在的時間。

Q: What time is the TV show?

問題：那電視節目的時間是幾點？

(A) I have no idea.
(A) 我不知道。

(B) It's great.
(B) 它很棒。

(C) I love it.
(C) 我喜歡。

☆ have no idea (片語) 不知道

Q: It's 9:55 now.

問題：現在是九點五十五分。

(A) Oh, hurry up. We don't have much time.
(A) 噢，快點。我們時間不多了。

(B) That's cool.
(B) 那很酷。

(C) Don't mention it.
(C) 不用客氣。

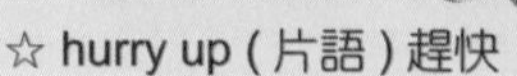

☆ hurry up (片語) 趕快

Let's Practice! 聽力練習

Q1

(A) It's at seven thirty.

(B) I also love it.

(C) Let's watch TV!

Q2

(A) It's February.

(B) It's my birthday.

(C) It's Saturday.

2-23 問「要多久時間」

TIPS:

MP3： L43-part2-23

「多久時間」的問句通常都是以 How long 或 How much time 開頭，回答時只要先看清楚選項，選表示「一段時間」的答案就對了。

A) Around two weeks

B) Next week

C) On Sunday

Q: How long will you stay there?

問題：你會在那裡待多久？

(A) 大約兩個禮拜。

(B) 下週。

(C) 在星期天。

學習重點

☆ stay (動) 待在…

☆ around (介) 大約

A) One hundred dollars

B) One hour

C) One hand

Q: How much time do you need to finish your homework?

問題：你完成回家作業要多久的時間？

(A) 一百塊錢。

(B) 一個小時。

(C) 一隻手。

學習重點

☆ finish (動) 完成

A) By airplane.

B) About two weeks.

C) It's beautiful there.

Q: How long will you stay in Paris?

問題：你會在巴黎待多久？

(A) 搭飛機。

(B) 大概兩週。

(C) 那裡很漂亮。

學習重點

☆ Paris (名) 巴黎

☆ airplane (名) 飛機

Let's Practice! 聽力練習

Q1

(A) Five hundred NT dollars.

(B) I am so excited.

(C) Around twenty minutes.

Q2

(A) In ten minutes.

(B) Tomorrow morning.

(C) About two weeks.

MP3： L44-part2-24

TIPS:
附和型的題目在英聽問答題中相當多，因為問題為直述句，回答前一定要先搞清楚句意的重點是什麼，再來決定選項中哪一個才是合理的附和回答。

(A) But you walk too fast.
(B) Yeah, it's very clear.
(C) I am coming.

Q: Do you follow me?
問題：你有聽懂我在說什麼嗎？
(A) 但你走太快了。
(B) 是的，非常清楚。
(C) 我來了。

學習重點
☆ follow (動) 跟隨
☆ Do you follow me?
意思就是「你有在跟著我說的內容聽嗎？」，衍生出來就是「你聽懂了嗎？」

(A) I will miss you so much.
(B) I will move it later.
(C) Good to see you!

Q: I will move to Hong Kong next month.
問題：我下個月要搬到香港。
(A) 我會很想念你。
(B) 我等一下會去搬它。
(C) 很高興見到你！

☆ miss (動) 想念

(A) You are thirsty.
(B) I love it as well.
(C) Are you happy?

Q: This doughnut is yummy!
問題：這甜甜圈真好吃！
(A) 你很口渴。
(B) 我也很喜歡。
(C) 你很開心嗎？

☆ doughnut (名) 甜甜圈
☆ thirsty (形) 口渴的
☆ as well (片語) 也…

Let's Practice! 聽力練習

Q1

(A) I live in Taipei.
(B) It looks comfortable.
(C) Do you like leaves?

Q2

(A) I will come.
(B) Yeah! I can't wait.
(C) Sorry. I can't come.

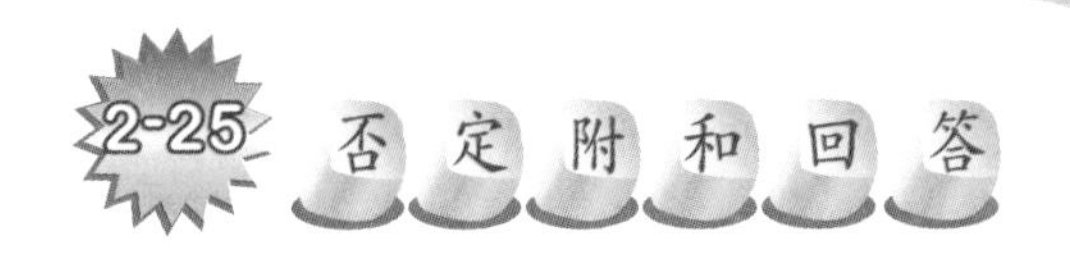

2-25 否定附和回答

MP3： L45-part2-25

TIPS:

和問題所描述的句子意思相反的否定附和題型，回答常會和題目句的語意相反，或是表示驚訝的問句，答題時同樣也是先聽清楚句意的重點是什麼，再來決定選項中哪一個才是合理的回答。

(A) What's wrong with you?

(B) Do you like hamburgers?

(C) It is a good idea.

Q: I don't want to go to school.

問題：我不想去學校。

(A) 你怎麼了？

(B) 你喜歡漢堡嗎？

(C) 那是個好主意。

☆ What's wrong…? [怎麼了？有哪裡不對勁？]

(A) Really? She didn't tell me.

(B) Where is she?

(C) I will go to Taipei tomorrow.

Q: She will move to Taitong next week.

問題：她下個禮拜會搬去台東。

(A) 真的嗎？她沒告訴我。

(B) 她在哪裡？

(C) 我明天會去台北。

題目的直述句表示的是一則消息，答題的重點就在於聽到這則消息後的反應。

(A) Do I have bad breath?

(B) That's too bad.

(C) I'm trying to cut down, but it isn't easy.

Q: Stop smoking! It's bad for your health.

問題：不要抽菸！它對你健康有害。

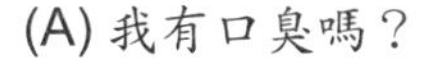

(A) 我有口臭嗎？

(B) 真不妙。

(C) 我正試著要戒掉，但並不容易。

☆ smoke（動）抽菸

☆ be bad for…（片語）對…有害

☆ bad breath（片語）口臭

☆ to cut down（片語）戒除

Let's Practice! 聽力練習

Q1

(A) That's great.

(B) It's a good idea.

(C) I'm sorry to hear that.

Q2

(A) You are a kind man.

(B) I'm terribly sorry.

(C) I wasn't lying on the bed then.

YOUR TURN! 實力挑戰題

1
(A) He is my father.
(B) He is handsome.
(C) He is a soldier.

Ⓐ Ⓑ Ⓒ

2
(A) It's one hundred NT dollars.
(B) My dad bought it for me yesterday
(C) It is cool, isn't it?

Ⓐ Ⓑ Ⓒ

3
(A) Is it good to drink?
(B) Do you need some sugar?
(C) It's really hot.

Ⓐ Ⓑ Ⓒ

4
(A) He comes here by train.
(B) It is coming.
(C) At eleven thirty.

Ⓐ Ⓑ Ⓒ

5
(A) It's delicious.
(B) He is fine.
(C) It's on the table.

Ⓐ Ⓑ Ⓒ

6
(A) We are cooks.
(B) I am her sister.
(C) We are going to the park.

Ⓐ Ⓑ Ⓒ

7
(A) She's really pretty.
(B) She's sitting there.
(C) She is my cousin, Linda.

Ⓐ Ⓑ Ⓒ

8
(A) It's really salty.
(B) OK. Here you are.
(C) Sorry, I don't have it.

Ⓐ Ⓑ Ⓒ

9
(A) I went there last night.
(B) Twice a week.
(C) It tastes good.

Ⓐ Ⓑ Ⓒ

10
(A) OK, I will.
(B) I have no cell phone.
(C) I am talking on the phone.

Ⓐ Ⓑ Ⓒ

GEPT 初級聽力 Starter

第三部份 簡短對話

簡短對話是英聽題型中難度較高的測驗。通常它會由兩個人對話構成一個情境。建議在答題前先看選項內容，聽題時仔細分辨情境，注意最後問題要問的是什麼。

範例題： M: Which one do you like, coffee or tea?

F : Coffee, please.

M: Do you want some sugar or milk?

F : No, thanks.

Q: What does the woman want?

(A) the coffee with milk

(B) the coffee with sugar

(C) the black coffee

正確答案為 (C)

TIPS:

MP3： L47-part3-1

問「說話者在說什麼」是很典型的對話類題型。這類題目要注意對話者在對話中所提供的資訊，通常會是一件事或是一樣東西，抓到關鍵字，選答案就不容易出錯。

M: How was your summer vacation?

F: I took a trip to Kenting with my family. It's so beautiful there.

M: That sounds nice. I'm planning to take a trip this weekend.

F: You must go there.

Q: What are the speakers talking about?

(A) The weather

(B) A trip

(C) Their family

男：你的暑假如何？

女：我和我的家人去墾丁旅行。那裡好漂亮。

男：聽起來很好。我這個週末也計劃要去旅行。

女：你一定要去那裡。

問題：說話者在談些什麼？

(A) 天氣

(B) 旅行

(C) 他們的家人

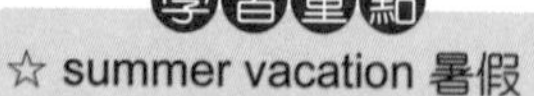

F: Is this book popular?

M: It's one of the best-selling books.

F: Jodi Picoult? Isn't she the writer of 'My Sister's Keeper?'

M: Yes, and this is her third novel.

Q: What are the man and the woman talking about?

(A) A housekeeper

(B) A book

(C) Two sisters

女：這本書很流行嗎？

男：這是暢銷書的其中一本。

女：茱蒂皮考特？她不是「姊姊的守護者」的作者嗎？

男：是的，而這本書是她的第三本小說。

問題：這男生和女生在談論什麼？

(A) 一位家庭主婦

(B) 一本書

(C) 兩位姊妹

學習重點

☆ popular (形) 流行的
☆ best-selling (形) 暢銷的

: How are you doing?

: I'm all done with the report.

: How long does it take you to finish?

: About two weeks.

: What is the woman saying?

(A) The woman has a lot of work to do.

(B) She wants to know what the man is doing.

(C) She has finished her report.

男：近來如何？

女：我終於把報告全做完了。

男：你花了多久時間完成？

女：大約兩個星期。

問題：這個女生在說什麼？

(A) 這個女生有很多工作要做。

(B) 她想要知道這個男生在做什麼。

(C) 她已經完成了她的報告。

☆ done (形) 完成了的
☆ report (名) 報告
☆ How long…? […要多久？]

 Let's Practice! 聽力練習

Q1

(A) A dog.

(B) A child.

(C) A road.

Q2

(A) Honey moon.

(B) Greece.

(C) America.

3-2 問「說話者正在做什麼」

TIPS: MP3：L48-part3-2

詢問「說話者正在做什麼」的題型，通常都會提供一個情境，除了聽清楚對話的內容外，還要注意對話者彼此之間的身份或關係，才不會選錯答案。

F: Is Peter there?

M: Who's speaking?

F: This is Helen. I'm his classmate.

M: Peter isn't at home now. I'll tell him to call you back.

Q: What is the man doing now?

(A) Doing the homework

(B) Talking on the phone

(C) Watching TV

女：彼得在嗎？

男：哪位找？

女：我是海倫。我是他的同學。

男：彼得現在不在家。我會跟他說要回電給你

問題：這個男人正在做什麼？

(A) 在做功課。

(B) 在講電話。

(C) 在看電視。

Ⓐ   B  Ⓒ

學習重點

☆ call 人 back
（片語）回某人電話

M: Could you give me a hand?

F: Sure. Is there anything I can do?

M: Please take three eggs from the refrigerator, put them in the bowl and mix with the flour.

F: OK.

Q: What are they doing?

(A) Cooking

(B) Buying eggs

(C) Doing dishes

男：你可以幫我個忙嗎？

女：當然。我可以做點什麼嗎？

男：請從冰箱裡拿三個蛋，把它們放到碗裡，然後和麵粉混合。

女：好的。

問題：他們在做什麼？

(A) 煮東西。

(B) 買雞蛋。

(C) 洗碗。

 A Ⓑ  Ⓒ

學習重點

☆ refrigerator（名）冰箱
☆ bowl（名）碗
☆ flour（名）麵粉
比較 flower（名）花朵
☆ to do the dishes（片語）洗碗

: How much is this digital camera?

: It's nine thousand dollars.

: Do you have a cheaper one?

: How about this blue one? It's only five thousand dollars.

: What is the woman doing?

(A) Buying cameras.

(B) Selling cameras.

(C) Fixing cameras.

男：這台數位相機多少錢？

女：它要九千元。

男：你有便宜一點的嗎？

女：這台藍色的如何？它只要五千元。

問題：這個女人在做什麼？

(A) 買相機。

(B) 賣相機。

(C) 修理相機。

☆ digital camera (名) 數位相機

☆ cheaper (形) 較便宜的

☆ fix (動) 修理

Let's Practice! 聽力練習

Q1

(A) Celebrating a birthday

(B) Making a birthday cake

(C) Buying birthday gifts

Q2

(A) Drinking coffee.

(B) Buying coffee.

(C) Making coffee.

3-3 問說話者想要、將要做什麼

TIPS:

MP3： L49-part3-3

問說話者「想要什麼」或「將要做什麼」的題型中，大多是朋友之間的對話，然後再問對話之後會進行的事，所以聽題目的重點要先分辨說話者「正在進行什麼動作」，才能判斷接下來會進行的動作。

M: What are you doing?

F : I am playing video games.

M: Can I join you?

F : Why not?

Q: Will the man play the video game with the woman?

(A) No, he won't.

(B) Yes, he will.

(C) We don't know.

男：你在做什麼？

女：我正在玩電動遊戲。

男：我可以加入嗎？

女：為什麼不，當然可以。

問題：這男生會和女生玩電動遊戲嗎？

(A) 不，他不會。

(B) 是的，他會。

(C) 我們不知道。

Ⓐ  Ⓒ

學習重點

☆ video games （名）電動遊戲

☆ join（動）加入

☆ Why not? 為什麼不？當然。

F: Let's go to the movies tonight ! I have two tickets.

M: Which movie are you going to see?

F : "Kung Fu Panda." It's very funny and meaningful.

M: That sounds good. Let's go!

Q: What are they going to do?

(A) Having dinner

(B) Seeing a movie

(C) Talking on the phone

女：我們今晚一起去看電影吧！我有兩張票。

男：你要去看什麼電影？

女：「功夫熊貓。」它很好笑而且很有意義。

男：聽起來不錯。我們去吧！

問題：他們要去做什麼？

(A) 吃晚餐。

(B) 看電影。

(C) 講電話。

Ⓐ  Ⓒ

學習重點

☆ ticket （名）票；罰單

☆ funny （形）搞怪的、好笑的

☆ meaningful （形）有意義的

F: Did Mike call yet?
M: Not yet, but I will let you know when he calls.
F: Thank you. I'm so worried about him. It's the first time he's taken a trip alone.
M: Take it easy. He'll be fine.
Q: What will the man do for the woman?
(A) He will take a trip alone.
(B) He will give Mike a call later.
(C) He will tell the woman when Mike calls.

女：麥克打來了嗎？
男：還沒，但他打來時我會讓你知道。
女：謝謝。我好擔心他。這是他第一次獨自去旅行。
男：放輕鬆。他會很好的。
問題：這個男人會幫那女人做什麼？
(A) 他會獨自去旅行。
(B) 他等一下會打電話給麥克。
(C) 當麥克打電話來時他會告訴那女人。

☆ Not yet. [尚未：還沒]
☆ Take it easy. [放輕鬆。]
☆ to give 人 a call (片語) 打電話給某人

Let's Practice! 聽力練習

Q1

(A) Yes, she will.
(B) No, she won't.
(C) She will give her a surprise.

Q2

(A) She will buy a new bike for him.
(B) She will find the way.
(C) She won't buy a new bike for him.

3-4 問說話者本身的訊息

TIPS:

MP3： L50-part3-4

回答「問說話者個人訊息」的題目，可以先看選項再聽題目。比較要小心的地方是男生和女生的身份可能不同，聽題的時候要聽清楚題目問的人是男生還是女生，或是對話者彼此間的關係與身份。

F: This is Room 1307. Can I order something?

M: Sure, what would you like?

F: I would like a bottle of wine.

M: Wait a moment, please.

Q: Who are the speakers?

(A) A hotel receptionist and a guest

(B) A waiter and a guest

(C) A boss and an employee

女：這裡是 1307 房。我可以點東西嗎？

男：當然，你想要點什麼？

女：我想要一瓶紅酒。

男：請稍待一下。

問題：說話的人是誰？

(A) 一位旅館接待員和一位客人。

(B) 一位餐廳服務生和一位客人。

(C) 一位老闆和一位僱員。

學習重點

☆ bottle (名) 瓶子
☆ Wait a moment. [請稍候]
☆ receptionist (名) 總機、接待人員
☆ guest (名) 客人
☆ waiter (名) 服務生
☆ boss (名) 老闆
☆ employee (名) 僱員；員工

M: Can you play the guitar?

F : No, I can't. Can you?

M: Yes, I can. I can teach you.

F : Really, that's great.

Q: Who can play the guitar?

(A) the woman

(B) the man

(C) the man and the woman

男：你會彈吉他嗎？

女：不，我不會。你會嗎？

男：是的，我會。我可以教你。

女：真的嗎？太棒了。

問題：誰會彈吉他？

(A) 女人。

(B) 男人。

(C) 男人和女人。

學習重點

☆ guitar (名) 吉他

M: How old are you?
F : Would you like to make a guess?
M: You look like a twenty-five-year-old woman.
F : Thank you. I'm thirty years old.
Q: How old is the woman?
(A) 25 years old
(B) 35 years old
(C) 30 years old.

男：你年紀多大？
女：你要猜猜看嗎？
男：你看起來像二十五歲的女生。
女：謝謝你。我三十歲了。
問題：這個女生幾歲？
(A) 25 歲。
(B) 35 歲。
(C) 30 歲。

Let's Practice! 聽力練習

Q1

(A) He is a baker.
(B) He is a waiter.
(C) He is a cook.

Q2

(A) He's a taxi driver.
(B) He's a bus driver.
(C) He's a clerk.

TIPS:

MP3：L51-part3-5

問說話者所在位置的題型，可先看選項給的內容再來聽題。通常選項中都會有表示位置的介系詞片語出現，所以先看選項再聽題目，很容易就能找到正確答案了。

M: Do you want to order now?
W: Yes, I want to have a meal number 3.
M: OK. What do you like to drink?
W: Coffee, please.
Q: Where are the speakers?
(A) In the supermarket.
(B) In the museum.
(C) In the restaurant.

男：您要點餐了嗎？
女：是的，我想要三號餐。
男：好的。您想要喝什麼？
女：請給我咖啡。
問題：說話者在哪裡？
(A) 在超市裡。
(B) 在博物館裡。
(C) 在餐廳裡。

學習重點
☆ supermarket（名）超市
☆ museum（名）博物館
☆ restaurant（名）餐廳

M: How do you feel now, Miss Lin?
W: I feel sleepy and have a runny nose.
M: Do you have a sore throat or headache?
W: I have a headache, and I might also have a slight fever.
Q: Where does the man work?
(A) In the restaurant.
(B) On the train.
(C) In the clinic.

男：林小姐，您現在覺得如何？
女：我想睡覺而且流鼻水。
男：你有喉嚨痛或頭痛嗎？
女：我頭痛，而且我可能也有點發燒。
問題：這個男人在哪裡工作？
(A) 在餐廳裡。
(B) 在火車上。
(C) 在診所裡。

Ⓐ  

☆ feel sleepy（片語）想睡覺
☆ to have a runny nose（片語）流鼻水
☆ to have a sore throat（片語）喉嚨痛
☆ headache（名）頭痛
☆ slight（形）輕微的
☆ fever（名）發燒

: Who is that girl?
: Which one?
: Look! She is standing under the tree.
: Oh, she is Nina. She is my sister.
: Where is Nina standing?
(A) in front of the bus stop
(B) under the tree
(C) next to the woman

男：那個女孩是誰？
女：哪一個？
男：看！她正站在那棵樹下。
女：哦，她是妮娜。她是我妹妹。
問題：妮娜站在哪裡？
(A) 在公車站牌前面。
(B) 在樹下。
(C) 在那女人的隔壁。

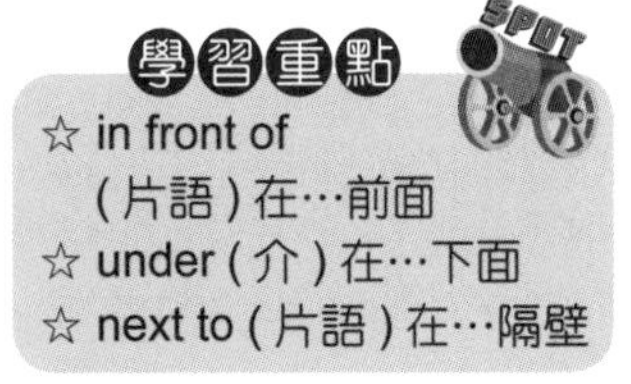

☆ in front of (片語) 在…前面
☆ under (介) 在…下面
☆ next to (片語) 在…隔壁

Let's Practice! 聽力練習

Q1

(A) In a pizza parlor.
(B) In a warehouse.
(C) In a grocery store.

Q2

(A) In the office.
(B) In the hospital.
(C) In the classroom.

TIPS:

MP3： L52-part3-6

問說話者要去哪裡的題型，結合了「將要做」和「在哪裡」兩種題型，聽題的重點要先釐清說話者所在的位置，通常較長的句子裡就是答案所在，所以聽到對話裡的長句子時要特別仔細聽清楚。

M: Where are you going, Nancy?
F : I am going to the cram school.
M: What? Do we have English class today?
F : Yes. Don't you remember that? Let's go quickly.
Q: Where are they going?

(A) They aren't going out together.
(B) They are going to the office.
(C) They are going to the cram school.

男：南西，你要去哪裡？
女：我要去補習班。
男：什麼？我們今天要上英文課嗎？
女：是啊。你不記得了嗎？我們趕快走吧。
問題：他們要去哪裡？

(A) 他們沒有要一起出去。
(B) 他們要去辦公室。
(C) 他們要去補習班。

Ⓐ  

學習重點
☆ cram school (名) 補習班
☆ quickly (副) 快點地

B: Do you feel better now?
G: No, I have a sore throat and a headache now.
B: You'd better see a doctor after school.
G: I will.
Q: Where will the girl go after school?

(A) The hospital.
(B) The restaurant.
(C) The school.

男孩：你現在有覺得好一點嗎？
女孩：不，我喉嚨痛而且頭痛。
男孩：你最好放學後去看個醫生。
女孩：我會的。
問題：這女孩放學後會去哪裡？

(A) 醫院。
(B) 餐廳。
(C) 學校。

Ⓐ  Ⓒ

☆ had better (片語) 最好

: Good morning, Angela. Where are you going?
男：早安，安琪拉。你要去哪裡？

': I'm going to work.
女：我要去上班。

: What? It's Sunday today.
男：什麼？今天是星期天耶。

':Our customers will visit us today, so I must be there.
女：我們客戶今天會拜訪我們，所以我必須去那裡。

: Where is the woman going to?
問題：這女人要去哪裡？

(A) The restaurant.
(B) The museum.
(C) The office.

(A) 餐廳。
(B) 博物館。
(C) 辦公室。

☆ customer (名) 客戶；顧客

 Let's Practice! 聽力練習

Q1

(A) a coffee shop
(B) a convenience store
(C) a bookstore

 Q2

(A) By the man's car.
(B) By bus.
(C) On foot.

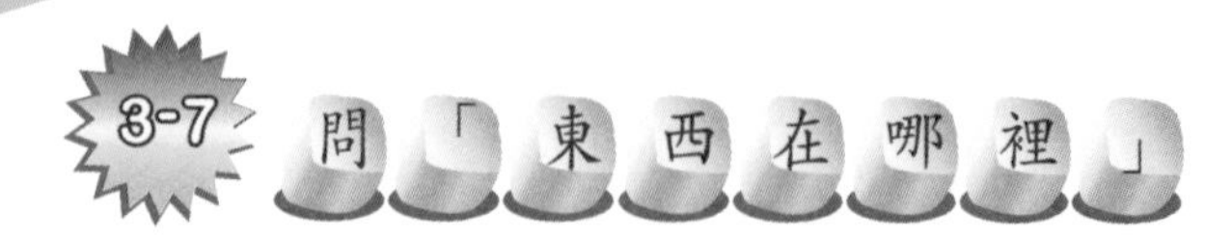

TIPS:　MP3：L53-part3-7

問「在哪裡」的題型同樣也可以從選項判斷出來，所以聽題前先看選項，看清楚答案中各種位置，再注意聽題目裡講到物品或人的所在位置，很快就能找到正確的答案了。

M: Did you see my watch?　男：你有看到我的手錶嗎？

F : Isn't it on your desk?　女：它不是在你的書桌上嗎？

M: No, I can't find it.　男：不，我找不到。

F : Here it is. It's under the desk.　女：這裡。它在你的書桌下面。

Q: Where is the watch?　問題：手錶在哪裡？

(A) On the desk　(A) 在書桌上。

(B) In the box　(B) 在盒子裡。

(C) Under the desk　(C) 在書桌下面。

☆ under (介) 在 ... 下面
☆ watch (名) 手錶

M: I am going to buy a new house.　男：我要買一間新房子了。

F : Where is your new house?　女：你的新房子在哪裡？

M: It's on Park Road and next to the coffee shop.　男：它在公園路上，一間咖啡館的隔壁。

F : Really? We are neighbors.　女：真的嗎？我們是鄰居呢。

Q: Where is the man's house?　問題：這個男生的房子在哪裡？

(A) It's on Park Road.　(A) 它在公園路上。

(B) It's next to the flower shop.　(B) 它在花店隔壁。

(C) It's between the park and the coffee shop.　(C) 它在公園和咖啡館的中間。

☆ neighbor (名) 鄰居

W: What are you looking for?
M: Did you see my key? I can't find it!
W: I saw it on your bed.
M: Really? Thanks a lot.
Q: Where is the man's key?
(A) On the woman's bed.
(B) On the man's bed.
(C) In the woman's hand.

女：你在找什麼？
男：你有看到我的鑰匙嗎？我找不到。
女：我看到它在你床上。
男：真的嗎？謝謝你。
問題：這個男人的鑰匙在哪裡？
(A) 在這個女人的床上。
(B) 在這個男人的床上。
(C) 在這個女人的手上。

學習重點
☆ to look for（片語）尋找

Let's Practice! 聽力練習

Q1

(A) Above the sofa.
(B) On the sofa.
(C) Under the sofa.

Q2

(A) In the boy's bag.
(B) On the desk.
(C) Under the desk.

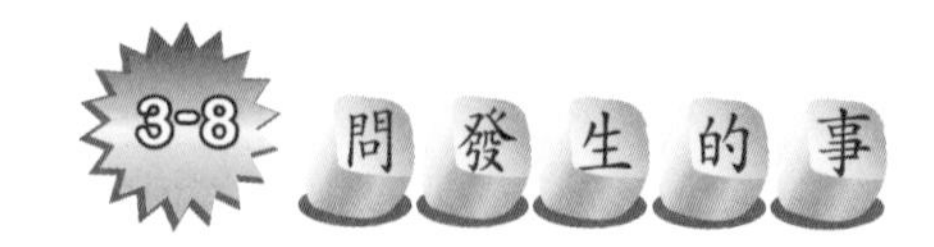

TIPS:

MP3：L54-part3-8

問「發生什麼事」的題型，聽題的重點在於對話者所講的事件內容，並且分辨清楚發生該事件的是男生還是女生，在回答時才不容易選錯。

M: What's wrong with your arm?
F : I sprained it this morning.
M: Are you OK now?
F : Yes, I feel much better now. Thanks.
Q: What's wrong with the woman?

(A) Her arm is hurt.
(B) She is sleepy.
(C) She is bored.

男：你的手臂怎麼了？
女：我今天早上扭傷了。
男：你現在還好嗎？
女：是的，我現在覺得好多了。謝謝。
問題：這個女生怎麼了？

(A) 她的手臂受傷了。
(B) 她想睡覺。
(C) 她覺得很無聊。

學習重點
☆ sprain（動）扭傷
☆ sleepy（形）想睡的
☆ bored（形）感到無聊的

F: Can you take out the garbage?
M: I'll do it later.
F: Please do it now. I can't stand the smell anymore.
M: Okay, I'll do it at once.
Q: Who will take out the garbage?

(A) the man
(B) the woman
(C) neither of them

A B C

女：你可以把垃圾拿出去丟嗎？
男：我等一下做。
女：請現在就做。我再也受不了這個味道了。
男：好吧，我馬上就做。
問題：誰會把垃圾拿出去丟？

(A) 男人。
(B) 女人。
(C) 他們兩個都不會。

學習重點
☆ garbage（名）垃圾
☆ smell（名）味道（動）聞起來
☆ anymore（副）再也…
☆ at once（片語）立刻
☆ neither（代）沒有（一個）；二者都不

M: Hey, look! It's my new T-shirt.
W: Oh, I can't believe it. I just bought the same one last week.
M: Really? I bought it in the night market yesterday. It's just NT$350.
W: Ha! But mine just cost me NT$300.
Q: What does the man find out?
(A) He spent less money buying the T-shirt.
(B) He and the woman bought the same T-shirt.
(C) The T-shirt is fashionable.

男：嘿，看吶！這是我的新T恤。
女：哦，我真不敢相信。我上個禮拜才買了件一模一樣的。
男：真的嗎？我昨天在夜市買的。它只要三百五十塊錢。
女：哈！但我的只花了三百塊錢。
問題：這個男生發現什麼？
(A) 他花了較少的錢買T恤。
(B) 他和那女生買了相同的T恤。
(C) 這件T恤很時尚。

☆ the same (片語) 相同的
☆ night market (名) 夜市
☆ cost (動) 花費
☆ fashionable (形) 時尚的

Let's Practice! 聽力練習

Q1

(A) Stayed at home
(B) Went fishing
(C) We don't know.

Q2

(A) He forgot to bring the English book.
(B) He found the English book.
(C) He didn't carry his bag.

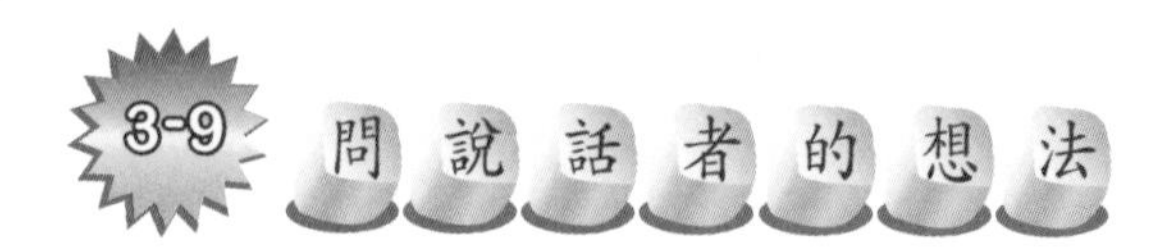

TIPS:

MP3：L55-part3-9

問「說話者想法」的對話屬於難度較高的題型。這類題目通常會是在討論一個事件或事物，所以聽題時要注意雙方對於這件事物的看法是否相同或相異，才不容易被選項誤導。

F: Did you see the movie last night?

M: Yes, I saw it with my girlfriend.

F: Did you like it?

M: Not really. It was so scary that my girlfriend kept screaming till the end.

Q: Did the man like the movie?

(A) No, he thought the movie was too scary.

(B) Yes, he thought the movie was exciting.

(C) No, his girlfriend didn't like it.

女：你昨晚有看那部電影嗎？

男：有，我和我女朋友一起去看了。

女：你喜歡嗎？

男：不。它太恐怖了，所以我女朋友一直尖叫個不停，直到電影結束。

問題：這個男生喜歡那部電影嗎？

(A) 不，他認為電影太恐怖了。

(B) 是，他認為電影很刺激。

(C) 不，他女朋友不喜歡。

Ⓐ Ⓑ Ⓒ

學習重點

☆ so…that+ 子句 [太…以致於…]

☆ scream (動) 尖叫

☆ end (名) 結束

☆ scary (形) 嚇人的

M: Can you help me clean my room?

F: Sure, where should I begin?

M: Please vacuum the floor and clean the table first.

F: No problem.

Q: What does the woman want?

(A) The woman wants the man to clean her room.

(B) The woman wants to vacuum the floor.

(C) She wants to know where she should clean first.

男：你可以幫忙我清理我房間嗎？

女：當然，我要從哪裡開始？

男：請先把地板吸一吸並清理餐桌。

女：沒問題。

問題：這女生想要什麼？

(A) 這女生想要這男生幫她清理她的房間。

(B) 這女生想要去吸地板。

(C) 她想知道她應該先從哪裡開始清理。

Ⓐ Ⓑ 

學習重點

☆ vacuum (動)(用真空吸塵器)吸

F: Can Joe cook good food?
M: Joe is an amazing cook!
F: I didn't know that. Can he cook Chinese food, too?
M: Sure, he makes the best Mapotofu in the world.
Q: What does the man think of Joe?
(A) He has no idea about Joe.
(B) Joe only cooks Chinese food.
(C) Joe cooks very well.

女：喬會煮好吃的菜嗎？
男：喬是個令人驚豔的廚師！
女：我從不知道這件事。他也會煮中國菜嗎？
男：當然，他做的麻婆豆腐是全世界最棒的。
問題：這個男人認為喬如何？
(A) 他不認識喬。
(B) 喬只會煮中國菜。
(C) 喬煮得很棒。

Let's Practice! 聽力練習

Q1

(A) Yes, he likes it very much.
(B) No, he didn't have any money.
(C) No, he thinks the shape is ugly.

Q2

(A) It's cheap.
(B) It's nice.
(C) It's expensive.

TIPS:

MP3：L56-part3-10

問「原因」和問「發生的事」的題型，兩者的答案選項看起來很像，都是完整的敘述句，這類型的題目要注意對話者談論的事情是什麼，才能找到正確的答案。

M: I'm so worried.
F : What's going on?
M: My puppy is sick.
F : Don't worry! It will get better.
Q: Why is the man so worried?
(A) His dog is sick.
(B) He is sick.
(C) His dad is sick.

男：我好擔心。
女：發生什麼事？
男：我的小狗生病了。
女：別擔心！牠會好起來的。
問題：為什麼這個男人很擔心？
(A) 他的狗生病了。
(B) 他生病了。
(C) 他的爸爸生病了。

A B 

學習重點
☆ puppy（名）小狗
☆ worried（形）擔心的

M: Can anyone spell "wonderful?"
F: Yes, I can. "W-O-N-D-E-R-F-U-L"
M: Good! Here is your prize.
F: Thank you, Mr. Li.
Q: Why does the girl get a prize?
(A) She is polite.
(B) She spells the word right.
(C) She has a wonderful day.

男：有誰會拼「wonderful」這個字？
女：是的，我會。W-O-N-D-E-R-F-U-L。
男：很好！這是你的獎品。
女：謝謝你，李老師。
問題：為什麼這個女孩得到了獎品？
(A) 她很有禮貌。
(B) 她拼對了這個字。
(C) 她有很棒的一天。

A  

學習重點
☆ spell（動）拼字
☆ wonderful（形）很棒的
☆ prize（名）獎勵
☆ polite（形）有禮貌的

W: You look so tired. What's up?
M: I stayed up working last night.
W: No wonder you keep yawning.
Q: Why is the man so tired?
(A) He is sick.
(B) He stayed up last night.
(C) He got a new job.

女：你看起來很疲倦。發生什麼事了？
男：我昨晚熬夜工作。
女：難怪你一直打呵欠。
問題：為什麼這個男生很疲倦？
(A) 他生病了。
(B) 他昨晚熬夜。
(C) 他找到一份新工作。

學習重點 SPOT
☆ tired（形）疲倦的
☆ to stay up（片語）熬夜
☆ No wonder…［難怪］
☆ yawn（動）打呵欠

Let's Practice! 聽力練習

Q1

(A) They are not good friends.
(B) He loves the cup.
(C) He broke the woman's favorite cup.

Q2

(A) She can't catch the bus.
(B) She is speaking.
(C) She is sick.

3-11 和時間有關的對話

TIPS: MP3：L57-part3-11

和時間有關的題型，從選項就可以判斷出來，唯一要注意的地方是對話者可能會提到兩、三個不同的時間點，要注意題目問的是何者，才能找出正確的答案。

M: Why have you come to my house?
W: You told me you would hold a party at noon, didn't you?
M: Didn't you receive my e-mail? The party will be at seven tonight.
W: Oh, I didn't check my e-mail box.
Q: When will the party begin?
(A) At twelve.
(B) At seven.
(B) At noon.

男：為什麼你到我家來了？
女：你跟我說你中午要辦個派對，不是嗎？
男：你沒收到我的電子郵件嗎？派對在今晚七點。
女：噢，我沒有檢查我的電子郵件。
問題：這個派對何時開始？
(A) 在十二點。
(B) 在七點。
(C) 在中午。

A  C

學習重點
☆ to hold a party （片語）舉辦派對
☆ receive （動）收到
☆ check （動）檢查
☆ begin （動）開始

W: Julia and I will see a movie at six. Would you like to go with us?
M: I would like to, but I have to work until seven.
W: That's OK. Julia and I will have dinner first, and then we'll see the movie at seven thirty.
M: That's fine. I will be at the movie theater before seven thirty.
Q: When will the speakers see a movie?
(A) At six.
(B) At seven.
(C) At seven thirty.

女：茱莉亞和我要去看六點的電影。你要跟我們一起去看嗎？
男：我很想去，但我得一直工作到七點。
女：那沒關係。茱莉亞和我會先吃晚飯，然後我們會去看七點半的電影。
男：那很好。我會在七點半之前抵達電影院。
問題：說話者幾點會去看電影？
(A) 六點。
(B) 七點。
(C) 七點半。

學習重點
☆ theater（名）電影院

: It's seven thirty. Hurry up, or we will be late.

: What are you talking about? We still have one hour.

: Don't we have to arrive at the school at eight o'clock?

: No, it's eight thirty.

: When should they arrive at the school?

(A) At seven thirty.

(B) At eight o'clock.

(C) At eight thirty.

男：現在是七點三十分。快點，不然我們要遲到了。

女：你在說什麼？我們還有一個小時的時間。

男：我們不是要八點到學校嗎？

女：不，是八點三十分。

問題：他們應該要幾點到學校？

(A) 七點三十分。

(B) 八點。

(C) 八點三十分。

Let's Practice! 聽力練習

Q1

(A) Tomorrow morning.

(B) Tomorrow afternoon.

(C) Tomorrow evening.

Q2

(A) At nine.

(B) At eight.

(C) At seven.

TIPS: MP3： L58-part3-12

和數字有關的題型與時間類的題型很像，也是從選項中就看得出來，通常對話都和買賣東西有關，注意題目問的是哪一個數字，很容易就可以選出正確的答案。

M: How much is the cap?
F : It's five hundred dollars.
M: Can you give me a discount?
F : Sorry, it's one price for all.
Q: How much is the cap?
(A) 500 dollars
(B) 450 dollars.
(C) 100 dollars.

男：這頂運動帽多少錢？
女：它要五百塊錢。
男：可以給我打個折嗎？
女：抱歉，不二價。
問題：這頂運動帽多少錢？
(A) 五百塊錢。
(B) 四百五十塊錢。
(C) 一百塊錢。

A B 

學習重點
☆ discount（名）折扣
☆ one price for all（片語）不二價

M: When did you begin learning the piano?
W: I have been practicing the piano since I was six years old.
M: Wow! Do you mean you have been practicing piano for ten years?
W: That's right. I love playing the piano so much.
Q: How old is the young lady?
(A) She's six years old.
(B) She's ten years old.
(C) She's sixteen years old.

男：你何時開始學琴的？
女：我從六歲就開始練琴了。
男：哇！你的意思是說你已經練琴練了十年了嗎？
女：沒錯。我很喜歡彈鋼琴。
問題：這個年輕女孩幾歲了？
(A) 她六歲。
(B) 她十歲。
(C) 她十六歲。

A  

M: My I help you?

W: Yes, I would like two hamburgers, one Coke and a glass of orange juice.

M: OK, two hamburgers, one coffee and a glass of orange juice.

W: No, it's Coke, not coffee.

Q: What does the woman order?

(A) Two hams, a cup of coffee and a glass of orange juice.

(B) Two hamburgers, one Coke and a glass of orange juice.

(C) Two fries, a cup of coffee and a glass of orange juice.

男：我能幫您嗎？

女：好的，我想要兩個漢堡，一個可樂和一杯柳橙汁。

男：好的，兩個漢堡，一杯咖啡和一杯柳橙汁。

女：不，是可樂，不是咖啡。

問題：這個女人點了什麼？

(A) 兩個火腿，一杯咖啡和一杯柳橙汁。

(B) 兩個漢堡，一杯可樂和一杯柳橙汁。

(C) 兩份薯條，一杯咖啡和一杯柳橙汁。

☆ hamburger (名) 漢堡
☆ ham (名) 火腿
☆ fries (名) 薯條
(= French fries)

Let's Practice! 聽力練習

Q1

(A) 350 dollars

(B) 250 dollars

(C) 150 dollars

Q2

(A) 0923-052-041

(B) 0923-025-014

(C) 0923-052-014

MP3：L59-part3-13

TIPS:
問「對與錯」的題型，選項通常會是完整的敘述句，答題前最好先看完選項再聽題目，比較容易掌握對話的人在說些什麼；此外，聽題時也要注意問題問的是 True 或是 Not True，才不會聽懂對話內容卻又選錯答案。

M: Which one do you like, strawberries or bananas?
F : I hate both of them. I like durian.
M: Yuck! I hate its smell.
F : Believe me, it's really yummy. You should try it.
Q: Which one is TRUE about the woman?
(A) She loves both strawberries and bananas.
(B) She hates fruits.
(C) She doesn't love strawberries or bananas.

男：你喜歡一種，草莓還是香蕉？
女：這兩個我都討厭。我喜歡榴槤。
男：噁心！我討厭它的氣味。
女：相信我，它真的很好吃。你應該試試看的。
問題：關於這個女人何者為真？
(A) 她草莓和香蕉都喜歡。
(B) 她討厭水果。
(C) 她不愛草莓或和香蕉。

☆ strawberry（名）草莓
☆ durian（名）榴槤
☆ yuck（感嘆詞）噁心（表示反感）
☆ yummy（形）美味的

W: She's so cute. Is she your daughter?
M: No, she's my sister, Emily.
W: Really? How old is she?
M: She's five years old.
Q: Which one is Not true?
(A) Emily is the man's sister.
(B) Emily is the man's daughter.
(C) The woman thinks Emily is cute.

女：她好可愛。她是你女兒嗎？
男：不，她是我妹妹，艾蜜莉。
女：真的嗎？她幾歲？
男：她五歲。
問題：哪一個不是真的？
(A) 艾蜜莉是這個男人的妹妹。
(B) 艾蜜莉是這個男人的女兒。
(C) 這個女人覺得艾蜜莉很可愛。

學習重點
☆ daughter（名）女兒

: Excuse me. Do you know how to get to the National Palace Museum?

: You can take Bus 30 and get off at the National Palace Museum stop.

How much is the bus ticket?

: It is $15.

Thanks for your help.

: Which one is NOT true?

(A) The woman will take the MRT.

(B) The price of the bus ticket is $15.

(C) The man knows how to get to the National Palace Museum.

女：抱歉。你知道怎麼樣去故宮博物院嗎？

男：你可以搭三十號公車，然後在故宮博物院站下車。

女：公車票要多少錢？

男：要十五元。

女：謝謝你的幫忙。

問題：哪一個不是真的？

(A) 這個女人會去搭捷運。

(B) 公車的票價是十五元。

(C) 這個男人知道如何去故宮博物院。

☆ National Palace Museum (名) 故宮博物院
☆ to get off (片語) 下車
☆ price (名) 價格

簡短對話

 Let's Practice! 聽力練習

Q1

(A) He is going to America tomorrow.

(B) He will go to America next year.

(C) He will stay in America for two years.

Q2

(A) The man is in front of the Taipei 101.

(B) The woman doesn't speak English.

(C) The woman is glad to help the man.

YOUR TURN! 實力挑戰題

MP3： L60-part3- 實力挑戰題

1
(A) The boss made the woman go home.
(B) The boss made the woman work on Sunday.
(C) The woman made the boss work with her on Sunday.

Ⓐ Ⓑ Ⓒ

2
(A) She forgot his birthday.
(B) She forgot their anniversary.
(C) She didn't remember the surprise.

Ⓐ Ⓑ Ⓒ

3
(A) Bill is Gina's brother.
(B) Bill is Mandy's brother.
(C) Gina is Bill's friend.

Ⓐ Ⓑ Ⓒ

4
(A) He is turning off the TV.
(B) He is playing basketball.
(C) He is watching a basketball game on TV.

Ⓐ Ⓑ Ⓒ

5
(A) By bus.
(B) By train.
(C) By taxi.

Ⓐ Ⓑ Ⓒ

6
(A) The girl went to a movie.
(B) She turned on the radio when she studied.
(C) She turned off the radio when she studied.

Ⓐ Ⓑ Ⓒ

7
(A) In the toy store.
(B) In the flower shop.
(C) In the restaurant.

Ⓐ Ⓑ Ⓒ

8
(A) Go to the library.
(B) Buy some books.
(C) Watch TV.

Ⓐ Ⓑ Ⓒ

9
(A) He is too excited.
(B) He is going to have his piano concert.
(C) He is going to the piano concert.

Ⓐ Ⓑ Ⓒ

10
(A) Yes, she will.
(B) No, she won't.
(C) Yes, she won't.

Ⓐ Ⓑ 

GEPT 初級聽力 Starter

第四部份 短文聽解

短文聽解雖然題目唸的內容很長，但其實難度並不會太高，主要還是測驗考生對圖片內容敘述的理解。它的題目通常在一開始就會先唸出來，所以答題時只要順著內容尋找符合答案的線索，很快就能找到正確的答案了。

範例題： Please look at the following three pictures.

Listen to the following message for Fred. What will Candy probably have for dinner?

Fred, this is Candy, would you like to come to my house for dinner? Amy and Jeff are both here. We're going to have pizza and watch a DVD together. Hope you could join us. Call me back as soon as possible.

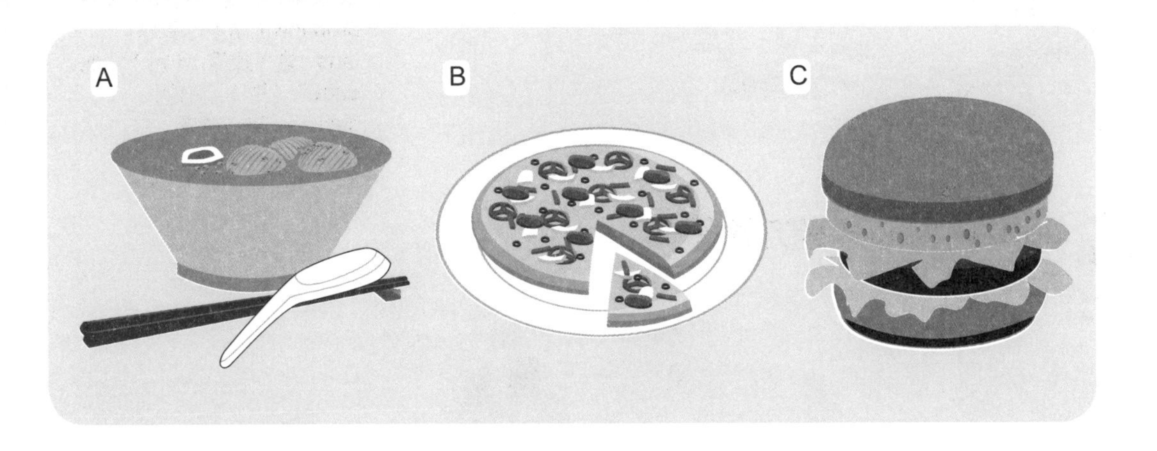

正確答案為 (B)

TIPS: MP3：L61-part4-1

短文聽解類的聽力題型，測驗的是對短文的理解，答題的重點在於問題問的內容，所以只要大概理解短文的情境或描述的事物，要選出正確答案並不困難。「公開場合廣播」是常會遇到的題目類型，這類題目大多為交通工具內或站內的廣播，或是商店賣場的廣播，掌握廣播的情境，答題就很容易了。

Please look at the following three pictures.

Listen to the following announcement. Where would you probably hear it?

We have landed at Cheer International Airport. The local time is 9:30 a.m. The current weather 15℃ . Thank you for choosing Hoping Airlines. We hope to see you soon!

請看接下來的圖片。

注意聽接下來的廣播。你可能會在哪裡聽到這段內容？

我們已經降落在奇耳國際機場。本地時間為上午九點三十分。目前氣溫為攝氏 15 度。感謝您選擇和平航空。希望能很快再見到您！

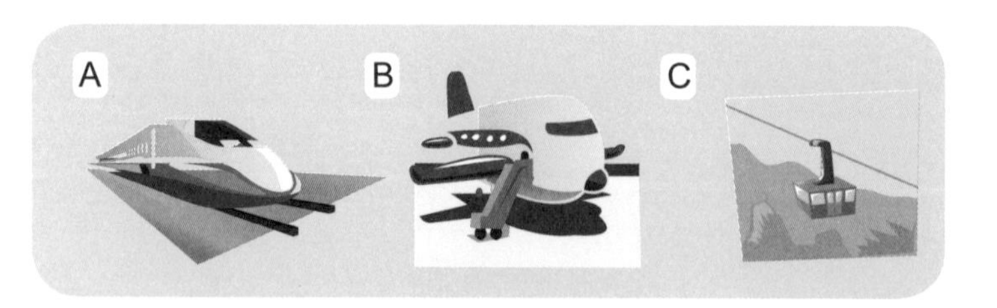

學習重點

☆ announcement (名) 廣播；宣佈
☆ announce (動) 宣佈；廣播
☆ probably (副) 可能地
☆ land (動) 降落；(名) 土地
☆ current (形) 目前的
☆ choose (動) 選擇

Let's Practice! 聽力練習

Q1

A

B

C

'lease look at the following three pictures.

isten to the following announcement. Where will you most probably hear it?

ttention all customers. We are offering a special discount on many kinds of cake today. The cheese ake is 10% off, the chocolate cake is 15% off, and other flavors are 5% off. If you buy five pieces of ake, we will give you one piece for free. Don't miss this chance.

青看接下來的三張圖片。

主意聽接下來的廣播。你最可能會在哪裡聽到這段內容？

各位顧客請注意。我們今天許多種類的蛋糕都有提供特別折扣。起司蛋糕打九折，巧克力蛋糕八五折，其它口味則有九五折優惠。若您買五件蛋糕產品，我們會再送您一份免費產品。不要錯過這個機會。

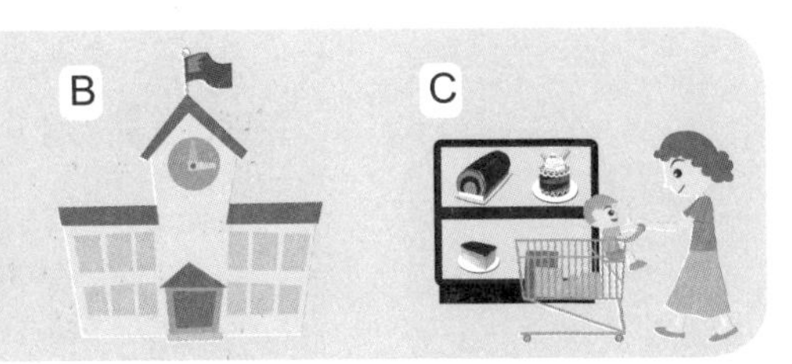

學習重點

☆ attention (名) 注意；(感嘆) 立正；注意
☆ customer (名) 顧客
☆ offer (動) 提供
☆ special (形) 特別的
☆ discount (名) 折扣
☆ flavor (名) 味道；口味
☆ chance (名) 機會

Let's Practice! 聽力練習

Q2

A  B  C 

短文聽解

TIPS:

MP3： L62-part4-2

留言類的題型可以分為答錄機留言及手機簡訊留言。這類題型要注意一開始時主要問題要問的是什麼，聽題時再依敘述的線索找出答案。

Please look at the following three pictures.

Tom left a message on Paul's answering machine. Where will Tom go after work today?

Hello, Paul, this is Tom. Peter told me that you're on sick leave. Are you OK now? Did you see a doctor? Peter and I are going to visit you after work. Do we need to bring dinner or anything for you? Call me back.

請看接下來的三張圖片。

湯姆在保羅的答錄機裡留了一則訊息。湯姆今天下班後會去哪裡？

哈囉，保羅，我是湯姆。彼得跟我說你請病假了。你現在還好嗎？你有去看醫生嗎？彼得和我下班後會去探望你。我們需要幫你帶晚餐或是什麼東西嗎？請回我電話。

Ⓐ Ⓑ ●C

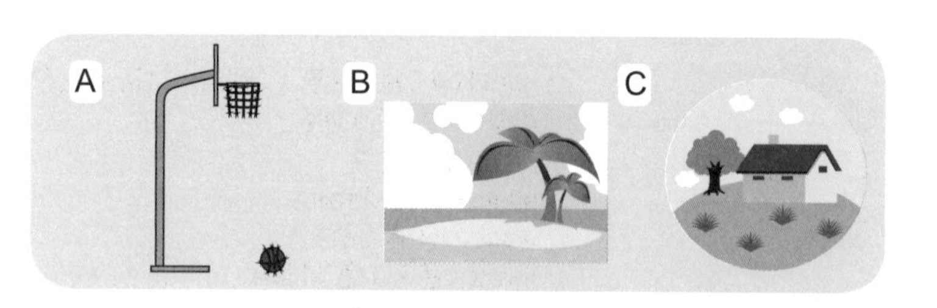

☆ leave (動) 留下；離開；(名) 請假
☆ on sick leave (片語) 請病假
☆ message (名) 訊息
☆ answering machine (名) 答錄機
☆ visit (動) 拜訪
☆ bring (動) 帶來

Let's Practice! 聽力練習

Q1

Ⓐ  

ease look at the following three pictures.

sten to the following message for Andy. What will Andy bring to Emily's house?

ndy, I left my cell phone at the office. Emily said that you will come to her party tonight. Could you ing the cell phone to the party for me? Thanks. See you at the party.

看接下來的三張圖片。

意聽接下來給安迪的訊息。安迪會帶什麼東西到艾蜜莉的家？

迪，我把我的手機留在辦公室了。艾蜜莉說你今晚會來她的派對。你可以幫我把手機帶到派對來嗎？謝。派對見。

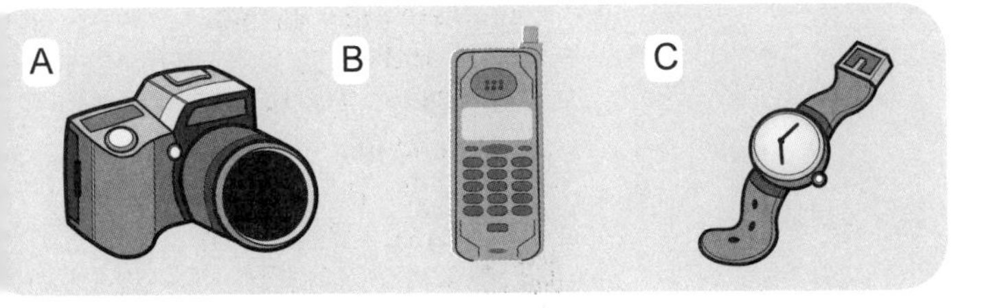

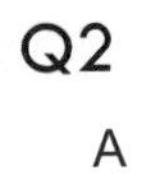

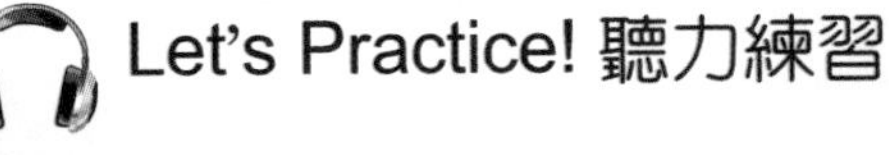

Let's Practice! 聽力練習

Q2

A

B

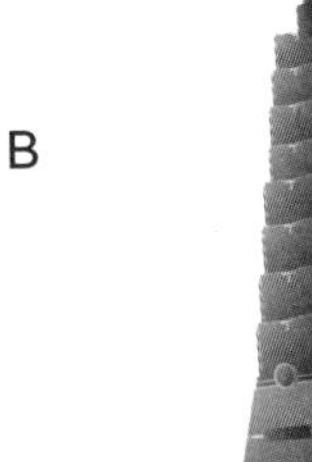

C

Ⓐ Ⓑ Ⓒ

短文聽解

TIPS: MP3： L63-part4-3

新聞氣象播報類的題型，聽題重點在先聽清楚題目要問的是什麼，接著再從敘述中尋找答案。這類題目的答題重點多半集中在比較後面的句子，所以要聽完全部的敘述再作答，以免被長段的內容誤導。

Please look at the following three pictures.

Listen to the following weather forecast. How will the weather be tomorrow in Taipei?

According to the Central Weather Bureau's forecast, it will get cold in northern Taiwan tomorrow. It w be the coldest November on record. The low temperature will drop to 10℃ at dawn in Danshui. Peopl who will go to this area must bring a heavy coat with them.

請看接下來的三張圖片。

注意聽接下來的氣象預報。明天台北的天氣如何？

根據中央氣象局的預報，明天北台灣會變冷。它會是有紀錄以來最冷的十一月。清晨的淡水低溫會降至攝氏十度。要到這個地方的人請隨身攜帶大外套。

學習重點

- ☆ weather forecast (片語) 天氣預報
- ☆ according to (片語) 根據
- ☆ Central Weather Bureau (名) 中央氣象局
- ☆ northern (形) 北部的
- ☆ on record (片語) 在紀錄上；有紀錄以來
- ☆ temperature (名) 溫度
- ☆ drop (動) 掉落；下降
- ☆ dawn (名) 清晨；黎明
- 比較 down (副) 往下
- 比較 at noon 在中午；at night 在晚上
- ☆ area (名) 地區；區域

Let's Practice! 聽力練習

Q1

Please look at the following three pictures.

Listen to this news story. What should people do if they bought old milk?

One brand of milk, United Cows Milk, has been selling milk that is too old. If you bought any United Cows Milk recently, please check the date on the bottle to see if the milk is past its expiration date. If you find that the milk is past the expiration date, just bring it back to the store, and you will get your money back.

請看接下來的三張圖片。

注意聽這個新聞報導。若人們買了過期牛奶應該要怎麼做？

有一個品牌的牛奶—聯合乳牛牛奶，賣出了過期許久的牛奶。若你最近有買任何一件聯合乳牛牛奶，請檢查瓶子上的日期看看是否已經過保存期限。如果你發現牛奶已過期，把它帶到商店，你可以拿回你的錢。

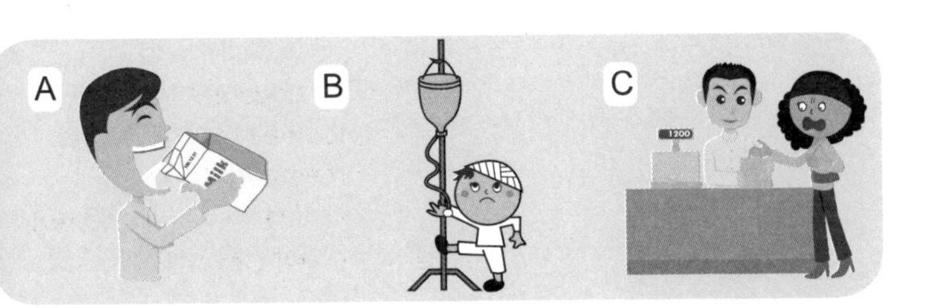

學習重點

☆ brand (名) 品牌
☆ recently (副) 最近
☆ expiration date (名) 有效期限

Let's Practice! 聽力練習

Q2

A

B

C

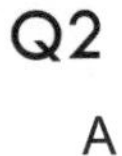

短文聽解

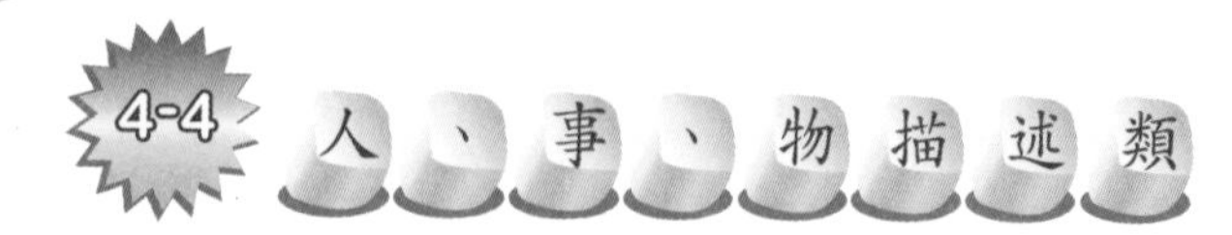

TIPS:

MP3：L64-part4-4

人事物描述類的題型，還是要先注意聽問題要問的是什麼，然後再依敘述中的內容找答案。有時敘述中會夾帶一些與主題相關、但與問題無關的訊息，所以聽題時一定要聽完全部的敘述後再作答。

Please look at the following three pictures.

Listen to the following short talk. What is David now?

David is good at sports. He started to play baseball when he was eight years old. After three years, he started to play football. In high school, he was a member of the school basketball team. Now, he is a professional golfer.

請看接下來的三張圖片。

注意聽接下來的短文。大衛現在是做什麼的？

大衛很擅長運動。他八歲開始打棒球。三年後，他開始打美式足球。在高中時，他是學校籃球隊的成員。現在，他是一位職業高爾夫球選手。

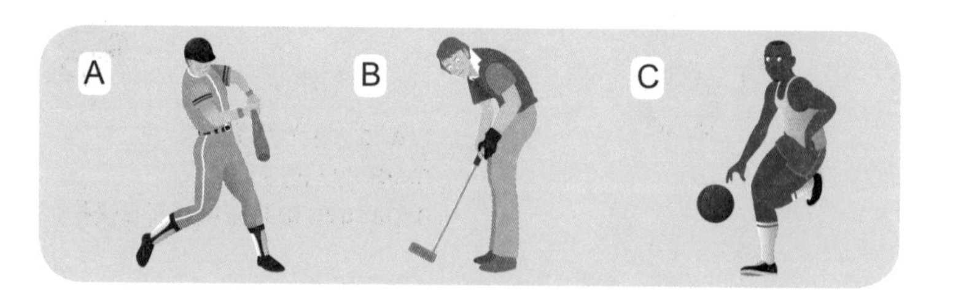

☆ be good at (片語) 擅長
☆ football (名) 美式足球
☆ member (名) 成員
☆ professional (形) 職業的
☆ golfer (名) 高爾夫球員

Let's Practice! 聽力練習

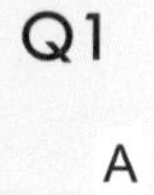

Q1

A

B

C

Ⓐ  

lease look at the following three pictures.

isten to the following short talk. What is Mandy most probably going to buy?

Iandy is going to make apple pie. She needs some apples, flour and eggs, but there aren't any apples t home. In order to make yummy apple pie, she is going to the supermarket.

青看接下來的三張圖片。

主意聽接下來的短文。曼蒂最有可能會去買什麼？

曼蒂要做蘋果派。她需要一些蘋果，麵粉及雞蛋，但家裡沒有任何蘋果了。為了要做美味的蘋果派，她要去超市了。

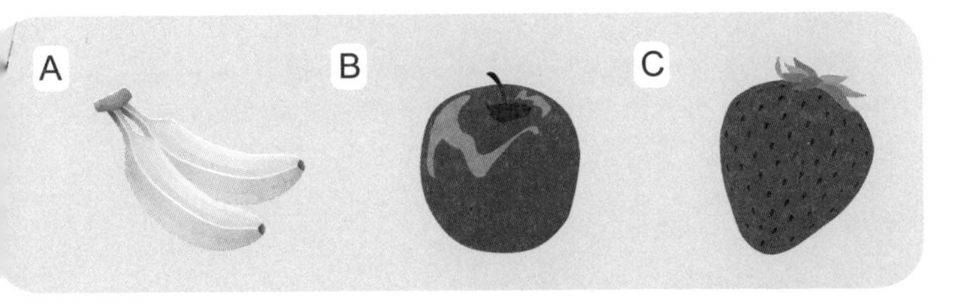

Let's Practice! 聽力練習

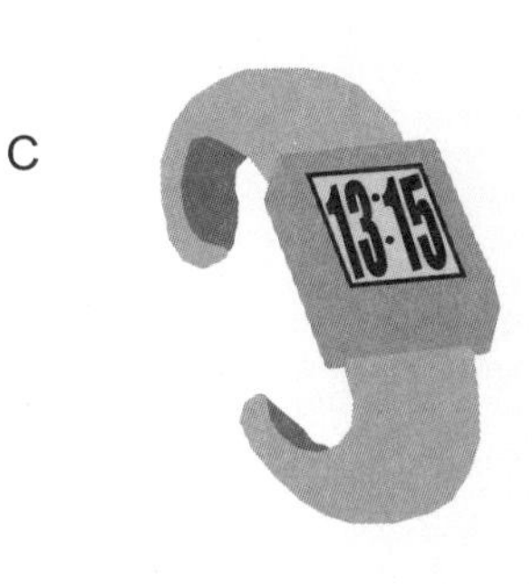

Ⓐ Ⓑ Ⓒ

YOUR TURN! 實力挑戰題

 MP3： L65-part4- 實力挑戰題

1

A 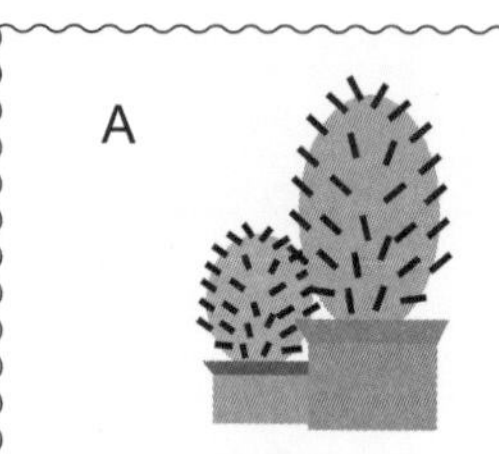
B 
C 

2

A 
B 
C 

Ⓐ Ⓑ Ⓒ

3

A 
B 
C 

4

A 
B 
C 

5

A 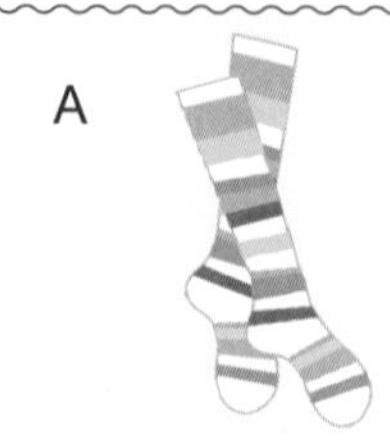
B 
C 

Ⓐ  

GEPT 初級聽力 Starter

學習成果測驗

學習成果測驗 PART 1 看圖辨義

 MP3：L66-學習成果測驗

Q1

Ⓐ Ⓑ Ⓒ

Q2

Ⓐ Ⓑ Ⓒ

Q3

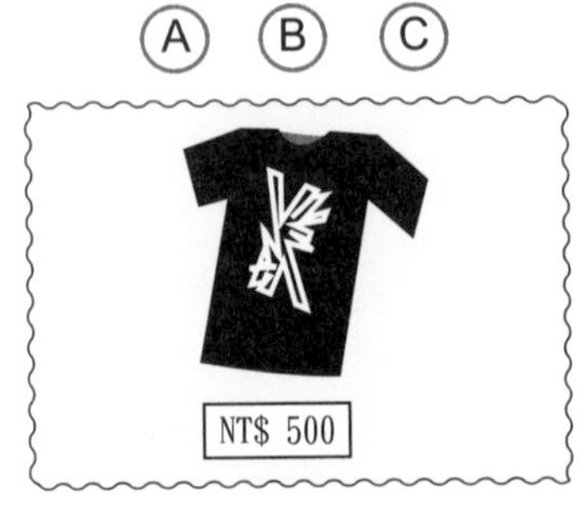

Ⓐ Ⓑ Ⓒ

Q4

Q5

學習成果測驗 PART 2 問答

Q1 Ⓐ Ⓑ Ⓒ

(A) Yes, it's mine. Thanks.

(B) I have a heavy coat.

(C) There is a jacket on the couch.

Q2 Ⓐ Ⓑ Ⓒ

(A) Sure. I also feel hot and stuffy.

(B) The air is fresh.

(C) Do you need some hot coffee?

Q3 (A) (B) (C) (A) I don't have a cell phone.
(B) Pardon? Could you please say it again?
(C) Wow! It's cool.

Q4 (A) (B) (C) (A) On Sunday.
(B) After dinner.
(C) Twice a month.

Q5 (A) (B) (C) (A) I am coming.
(B) We are going to leave.
(C) Oh, no! I will miss the train.

Q6 (A) (B) (C) (A) I have a lot of time.
(B) Yes, it's hot.
(C) Oh, no! Let's hurry up.

Q7 (A) (B) (C) (A) I was surfing on the Internet at that time.
(B) They will take a part-time job.
(C) We will go to the museum.

Q8 (A) (B) (C) (A) No, It's cool today.
(B) It's too bad.
(C) Take a rest and drink more water.

Q9 (A) (B) (C) (A) That's cool.
(B) I think we should wait for the next one.
(C) I need to go home.

Q10 (A) (B) (C) (A) Wow! It's pretty.
(B) I feel cold.
(C) We will go out.

學習成果測驗 PART 3 簡短對話

Q1 Ⓐ Ⓑ Ⓒ
(A) because he is making a detour.
(B) because there are so many cars on the road.
(C) because the man and the woman are too busy.

Q2 Ⓐ Ⓑ Ⓒ
(A) where he can buy a beautiful road.
(B) how long it will take to walk to Beauty Road.
(C) when he can walk.

Q3 Ⓐ Ⓑ Ⓒ
(A) On the airplane.
(B) In the restaurant.
(C) In the park.

Q4 Ⓐ Ⓑ Ⓒ
(A) 10 years old.
(B) 25 years old.
(C) 5 years old.

Q5 Ⓐ Ⓑ Ⓒ
(A) Buying some food for her son.
(B) Making a cake for her son.
(C) Buying the clothes for her son.

Q6 Ⓐ Ⓑ Ⓒ
(A) in the library.
(B) at the hotel.
(C) in the fast food restaurant.

Q7 Ⓐ Ⓑ Ⓒ
(A) Cleaning the house.
(B) Moving the tables.
(C) Watching TV.

Q8 Ⓐ Ⓑ Ⓒ
(A) Helen and Tom work together.
(B) Helen is talking on the phone.
(C) Tom and Helen live together.

Q9 (A) (B) (C) (A) In the men's room.
(B) On the bus.
(C) In the river.

Q10 (A) (B) (C) (A) The woman feels bad.
(B) The woman doesn't have a day.
(C) The man is sad.

學習成果測驗 PART 4 短文聽解

Q1

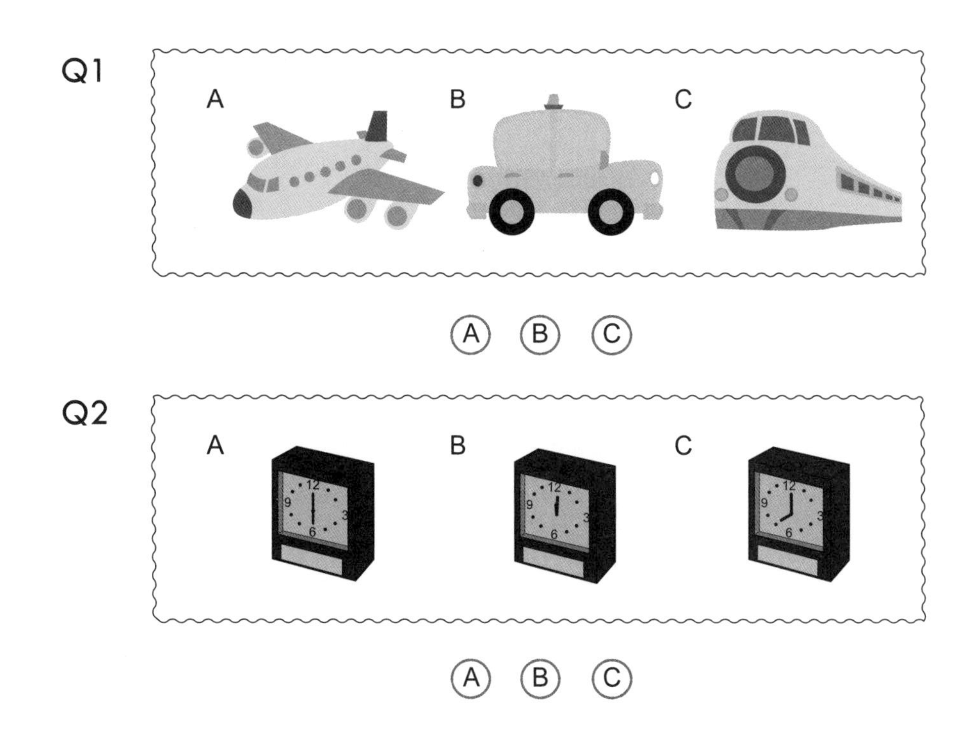

(A) (B) (C)

Q2

(A) (B) (C)

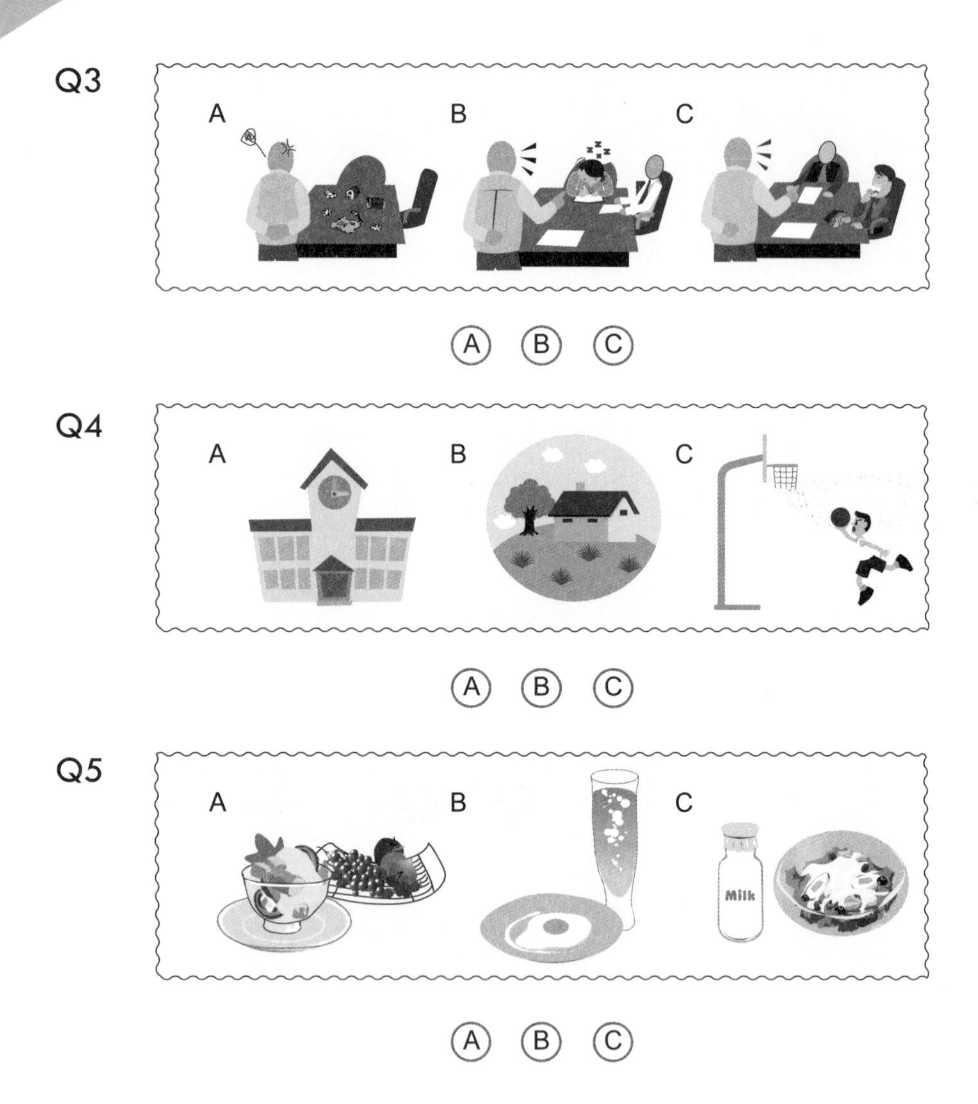
Q3
A
B
C
Ⓐ Ⓑ Ⓒ
Q4
A
B
C
Ⓐ Ⓑ Ⓒ
Q5
A
B
C
Milk
Ⓐ Ⓑ Ⓒ

GEPT 初級聽力 Starter

Answer Key

看圖辨義 PART 1-1 看鐘錶

Q1

Q: What time is it?

(A) It's five to seven.

(B) It's five after seven.

(C) It's seven past five.

問題：現在幾點？

(A) 現在差五分七點。

(B) 現在七點過五分。

(C) 現在五點七分。

Q2

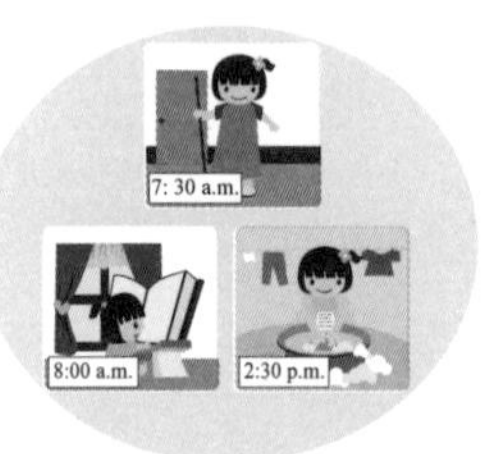

Q: What is the girl doing at eight o'clock?

(A) She's sweeping the room.

(B) She's washing the clothes.

(C) She's reading books.

問題：這個女孩在八點時在做什麼？

(A) 她正在掃房間。

(B) 她正在洗衣服。

(C) 她正在讀書。

看圖辨義 PART 1-2 看日期

Q1

Q: When does the old man go to the hospital?

(A) On Saturday.

(B) On April, 8th.

(C) In December.

問題：這位老先生何時要去醫院？

(A) 在星期六。

(B) 在四月八日。

(C) 在十二月。

Q2

Q: What does the man do on Sunday?

(A) Play football.

(B) Play baseball.

(C) Play golf.

問題：這個男人在星期日做什麼？

(A) 踢足球。

(B) 打棒球。

(C) 打高爾夫球。

看圖辨義 PART 1-3 問天氣

Q1

Q: How is the weather?

(A) It is cloudy.

(B) It is rainy.

(C) It is sunny.

問題：天氣如何？

(A) 現在雲很多。

(B) 現在下雨。

(C) 現在天晴。

Q2

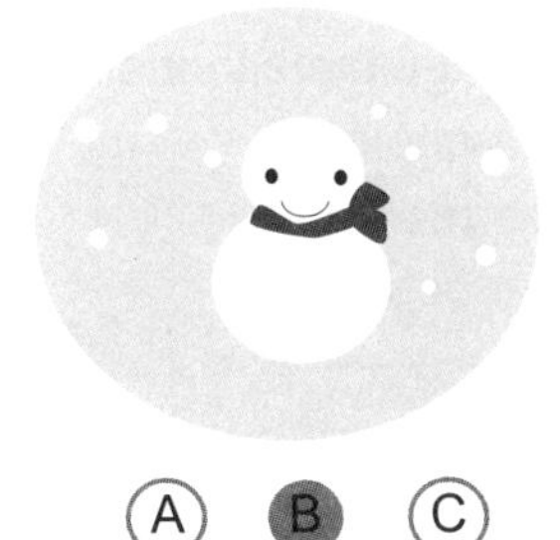

Q: What is the weather like?

(A) It's cool and windy.

(B) It's cold and snowy.

(C) It's hot and sunny.

問題：天氣怎麼樣？

(A) 現在涼爽風又大。

(B) 現在冷又下雪。

(C) 現在熱又晴朗。

看圖辨義 PART 1-4 問月份或季節

Q1

Q: What month is it?

(A) December

(B) September

(C) August

問題：這是哪一個月？

(A) 十二月。

(B) 九月。

(C) 八月。

Q2

Q: What kind of occasion is it?

(A) Graduation.

(B) Wedding.

(C) Funeral.

問題：這是什麼場合？

(A) 畢業。

(B) 結婚。

(C) 葬禮。

看圖辨義 PART 1-5 問數量

Q1

Q: How many glasses of juice are there?
(A) There are five glasses of juice.
(B) There are six glasses of juice.
(C) There are three glasses of juice.

問題：有多少杯果汁？
(A) 有五杯果汁。
(B) 有六杯果汁。
(C) 有三杯果汁。

Q2

Q: How many people are there in the house?
(A) There are six people.
(B) There are five people.
(C) There are four people.

問題：房子裡有幾個人？
(A) 有六個人。
(B) 有五個人。
(C) 有四個人。

看圖辨義 PART 1-6 問價格

Q1

Q: How much is the bag?
(A) $690
(B) $390
(C) $530

問題：這個包包多少錢？
(A) 690 元。
(B) 390 元。
(C) 530 元。

Q2

Q: How much does it cost to go from Taipei to Taichung?
(A) One hundred twenty-eight dollar.
(B) One hundred ninety-eight dollars.
(C) Nine hundred eighty-five dollars.

問題：從台北到台中要多少錢？
(A) 128 元。
(B) 198 元。
(C) 985 元。

看圖辨義 PART 1-7 問位置或地點

Q1

Q: Where is the boy?
(A) He is in the tree.
(B) He is under the tree.
(C) He is on the tree.

問題：這個男孩在哪裡？
(A) 他在樹上。
(B) 他在樹下。
(C) 他在樹頂。

Q2

Q: Where is the boy?
(A) He's sitting in front of the woman.
(B) He's kneeling down before the woman.
(C) He's standing in back of the woman.

問題：這個男孩在哪裡？
(A) 他坐在這個女人的前面。
(B) 他跪在那女人的前面。
(C) 他正站在那女人的後面。

看圖辨義 PART 1-8 問「是什麼」

Q1

Q: What are these?
(A) They are a ruler and an eraser.
(B) They are a comb and a mirror.
(C) They are high heels and lipsticks.

問題：這些是什麼？
(A) 它們是一把尺和一個橡皮擦。
(B) 它們是一把梳子和一個鏡子。
(C) 它們是高跟鞋和口紅。

Q2

Q: What is the animal on the right side?
(A) It's an octopus.
(B) It's a zebra.
(C) It's a butterfly.

問題：右邊的動物是什麼？
(A) 牠是隻章魚。
(B) 牠是一匹斑馬。
(C) 牠是一隻蝴蝶。

看圖辨義 PART 1-9 問「有什麼」

Q1

A B C

Q: What is behind the girl?

(A) A Christmas tree.

(B) A dinosaur.

(C) An umbrella.

問題：這個女孩的後面是什麼？

(A) 一棵聖誕樹。

(B) 一隻恐龍。

(C) 一把雨傘。

Q2

A B C

Q: What does the girl have?

(A) a dog

(B) a dinosaur

(C) an elephant

問題：這個女孩有什麼？

(A) 一隻狗。

(B) 一隻恐龍。

(C) 一隻大象。

看圖辨義 PART 1-10 問「人的狀態」

Q1

A  

Q: How can the child go to the kindergarten?

(A) by ship

(B) by airplane

(C) by school bus

問題：這個孩子如何去上學？

(A) 搭船。

(B) 搭飛機。

(C) 搭校車。

Q2

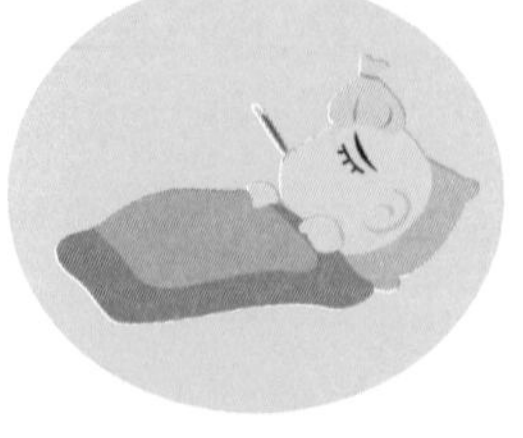

A  C

Q: What's wrong with the boy?

(A) He is angry.

(B) He caught a cold.

(C) He missed the bus.

問題：這個男孩怎麼了？

(A) 他生氣了。

(B) 他感冒了。

(C) 他錯過巴士了。

看圖辨義 PART 1-11 問「物品的狀態」

Q1

Q: What can we say about the tea?

(A) It's hot.

(B) It's bitter.

(C) It's cold.

問題：關於這杯茶我們能說什麼？

(A) 它是熱的。

(B) 它是苦的。

(C) 它是冷的。

Q2

Q: What can we say about the wine?

(A) It's hot.

(B) It's icy.

(C) It's sweet.

問題：關於這個酒我們能說什麼？

(A) 它是熱的。

(B) 它是冰的。

(C) 它是甜的。

看圖辨義 PART 1-12 問「人的外表」

Q1

Q: How does the woman look?

(A) Slim and charming.

(B) Chubby and ugly.

(C) Short and fat.

問題：這個女人看起來如何？

(A) 苗條又有魅力。

(B) 圓胖又醜。

(C) 又矮又胖。

Q2

Q: What is the girl wearing?

(A) She is wearing a T-shirt.

(B) She is singing.

(C) She is wearing a dress.

問題：這個女孩穿什麼？

(A) 她穿著一件T恤。

(B) 她正在唱歌。

(C) 她穿著一件洋裝。

看圖辨義 PART 1-13 問「人的情緒」

Q1

Q: What can we say about the boy?

(A) He feels happy.

(B) He is sick.

(C) He loves chocolate cake.

問題：關於這個男孩我們能說什麼？

(A) 他覺得開心。

(B) 他生病了。

(C) 他喜歡巧克力蛋糕。

Q2

Q: How does the boy feel?

(A) He feels sorrowful.

(B) He feels cheerful.

(C) He feels scared.

問題：這個男孩覺得如何？

(A) 他覺得悲傷。

(B) 他覺得振作了起來。

(C) 他覺得害怕。

看圖辨義 PART 1-14 問「人的嗜好」

Q1

Q: What is her hobby?

(A) singing

(B) crying

(C) speaking

問題：她的嗜好是什麼？

(A) 唱歌。

(B) 哭泣。

(C) 演說。

Q2

Q: What kinds of activities does the man do?

(A) Bungee jumping.

(B) Scuba diving.

(C) Surfing.

問題：這個男人在從事什麼活動？

(A) 高空彈跳。

(B) 潛水。

(C) 衝浪。

看圖辨義 PART 1-15 問「職業」

Q1

A  

Q: What is the man?
(A) He's a singer.
(B) He's a baseball player.
(C) He's a mailman.

問題：這個男人是做什麼的？
(A) 他是個歌手。
(B) 他是一位棒球選手。
(C) 他是一位郵差。

Q2

Q: What is the woman on the left side?
(A) She's a nurse.
(B) She's a cook.
(C) She's a reporter.

問題：左邊的女人是做什麼的？
(A) 她是一名護士。
(B) 她是一名廚師。
(C) 她是一位記者。

看圖辨義 PART 1-16 問「正在做什麼」

Q1

A B 

Q: What is the boy eating?
(A) He is eating at home.
(B) He is so happy.
(C) He is eating noodles.

問題：這個男孩在吃什麼？
(A) 他正在家吃東西。
(B) 他很開心。
(C) 他正在吃麵。

Q2

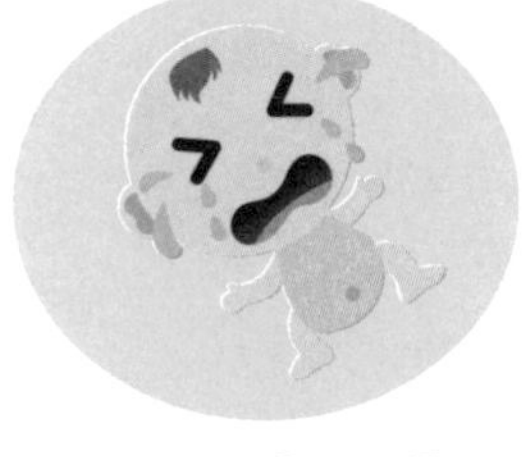

 B C

Q: What is happening in the picture?
(A) The baby is crying.
(B) The baby is laughing.
(C) The baby is crawling.

問題：圖片裡發生了什麼事？
(A) 這個小嬰孩在哭泣。
(B) 這個小嬰孩在笑。
(C) 這個小嬰孩在爬。

看圖辨義 PART 1-17 問「將要做什麼」

Q1

(A) (B) (C)

Q: What will the boy probably say?

(A) Merry Christmas!
(B) Happy New Year!
(C) Happy birthday!

問題：這個男孩可能會說什麼？

(A) 聖誕快樂！
(B) 新年快樂！
(C) 生日快樂！

Q2

(A) (B) (C)

Q: What will the boy probably do next?

(A) Play baseball.
(B) Play volleyball
(C) Play the flute.

問題：這個男孩接下來可能會做什麼？

(A) 打棒球。
(B) 打排球。
(C) 吹笛子。

看圖辨義 PART 1-18 問「何者為真」

Q1

(A) (B) (C)

Q: What is TRUE about the picture?

(A) They are reading a book.
(B) They are sleeping.
(C) They are playing the piano.

問題：關於這張圖片何者為真？

(A) 他們在讀一本書。
(B) 他們在睡覺。
(C) 他們在彈鋼琴。

Q2

(A) (B) (C)

Q: What's TRUE about the girl?

(A) She's standing on the ladder.
(B) She's playing volleyball.
(C) She's driving a car.

問題：關於這個女孩何者為真？

(A) 她正站在梯子上。
(B) 她正在打排球。
(C) 她正在開車。

看圖辨義 PART 1-19 問「何者不是真的」

Q1

Q: What is NOT true?

(A) Today is Christmas

(B) It is cold today.

(C) The girl is eating.

問題：何者不是真的？

(A) 今天是聖誕節。

(B) 今天很冷。

(C) 這個女孩正在吃東西。

Q2

Q: What is NOT true about the picture?

(A) She's a teacher.

(B) She's teaching English.

(C) She wears a pair of glasses.

問題：關於這張圖片何者不是真的？

(A) 她是一位老師。

(B) 她正在教英文。

(C) 她戴了一副眼鏡。

YOUR TURN! 實力挑戰題

Q1

Q: What is the weather like?

(A) It's cloudy.

(B) It rains heavily.

(C) It's hot today.

問題：天氣如何？

(A) 現在多雲。

(B) 現在下大雨。

(C) 今天很熱。

Q2

Q: What is the woman doing?

(A) Cleaning the window.

(B) Watering the flowers.

(C) Vacuuming the room.

問題：這個女人在做什麼？

(A) 清理窗戶。

(B) 澆花。

(C) 用吸塵器清理房間。

Q3

Q: What is NOT true about the picture?

(A) He is a clown.

(B) He is throwing balls.

(C) He is wearing a skirt.

問題：關於這張圖片何者有誤？

(A) 他是一個小丑。

(B) 他正在丟球。

(C) 他穿著裙子。

Q4

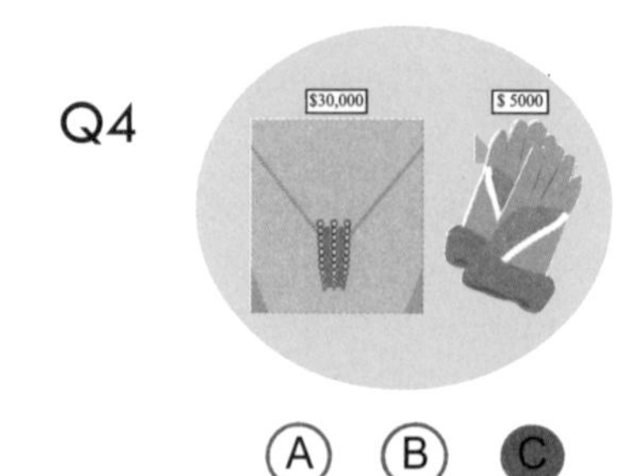

Q: What is NOT true about the necklace and the gloves?

(A) The necklace is more expensive than the gloves.

(B) The gloves are cheaper than the necklace.

(C) The necklace is three thousand dollars.

問題：關於這項鍊及手套何者有誤？

(A) 項鍊比手套貴。

(B) 手套比項鍊便宜。

(C) 項鍊要三千塊錢。

Q5

Q: Where is the man working?

(A) He's working in the high building.

(B) He's working in the gas station.

(C) He's working at home.

問題：這個男人在哪裡工作？

(A) 他在這棟大樓工作。

(B) 他在加油站工作。

(C) 他在家工作。

Q6

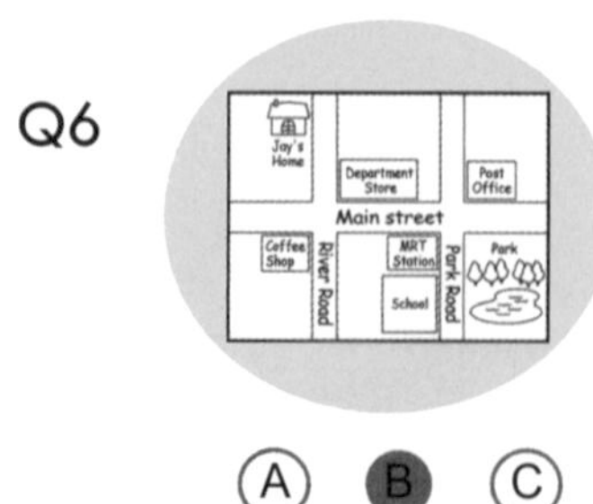

Q: Where is Jay's home?

(A) It's next to the post office.

(B) It's on River Road.

(C) It's in front of the park.

問題：杰的家在哪裡？

(A) 它在郵局隔壁。

(B) 它在河流路上。

(C) 它在公園前面。

Q: How much is the ice cream?
(A) $30
(B) $120
(C) $25

問題：冰淇淋要多少錢？
(A) 30 元。
(B) 120 元。
(C) 25 元。

Q: What is the man?
(A) a farmer
(B) a waiter
(C) a musician

問題：這個男人是做什麼的？
(A) 一位農夫。
(B) 一位服務生。
(C) 一位音樂家。

Q: What is there in the picture?
(A) A pair of sunglasses.
(B) A glass of lemonade.
(C) A bag of tomatoes.

問題：圖片裡有什麼？
(A) 一副太陽眼鏡。
(B) 一杯檸檬汁。
(C) 一袋蕃茄。

Q: When will Alice arrive at the airport?
(A) At three thirty.
(B) At five thirty.
(C) At seven thirty.

問題：艾莉絲何時會到機場？
(A) 在三點三十分。
(B) 在五點三十分。
(C) 在七點三十分。

問答 PART 2-1 日常招呼

Q1 Q: How are you today?
(A) I am pretty good.
(B) I feel cold.
(C) I am fifteen years old.

問題：你今天如何？
(A) 我很好。
(B) 我覺得冷。
(C) 我十五歲。

Q2 Q: Hey, what's new?
(A) Nothing much.
(B) No news is good news.
(C) The book is new.

問題：嘿，有什麼新鮮事嗎？
(A) 沒什麼特別的。
(B) 沒消息就是好消息。
(C) 這本書是新的。

問答 PART 2-2 表達讚美與祝福

Q1 Q: Your overcoat is so cool.
(A) Thank you.
(B) That's right.
(C) No, it's hot today.

問題：你的外套很酷。
(A) 謝謝。
(B) 沒錯。
(C) 不，今天很熱。

Q2 Q: Today is my birthday.
(A) Happy Birthday.
(B) That's great.
(C) Good luck!

問題：今天是我的生日。
(A) 生日快樂。
(B) 那很棒。
(C) 祝你好運！

問答 PART 2-3 感謝與致歉

Q1 Q: Sorry, I kept you waiting so long.
(A) I'm sorry to hear that.
(B) You're welcome.
(C) That's all right.

問題：抱歉，我讓你等這麼久。
(A) 我很遺憾聽到這個。
(B) 不客氣。
(C) 沒關係。

Q2 Q: Thank you for your help.
(A) Not at all.
(B) Nice to meet you.
(C) It's kind of you to say so.

問題：謝謝你的幫忙。
(A) 沒什麼。
(B) 很高興見到你。
(C) 你真好心這樣說。

問答 PART 2-4 電話用語

Q1 Q: Hello, is Benson there?
(A) There is Benson.
(B) Yes, he is there.
(C) Who is speaking?

問題：哈囉，班森在嗎？
(A) 有班森。
(B) 是的，他在那裡。
(C) 是哪位？

Q2 Q: Hello, is Jennifer there?
(A) I'm sorry. There is no one by that name.
(B) Nice to meet you!
(C) I'm here. May I help you?

問題：哈囉，珍妮佛在嗎？
(A) 抱歉。這裡沒有這個人。
(B) 很高興見到你！
(C) 我在這。有什麼我可以幫忙的嗎？

問答 PART 2-5 問數量與價格

Q1 Q: How many children are there in your family?
(A) Two.
(B) I have a girlfriend.
(C) My mom has two sisters.

問題：你家裡有幾個小孩？
(A) 兩個。
(B) 我有一個女朋友。
(C) 我媽媽有兩個姊妹。

Q2 Q: How much did you spend on the cake?
(A) Two hours.
(B) Last week.
(C) Five hundred NT dollars.

問題：你花了多少錢在蛋糕上？
(A) 兩個小時。
(B) 上個禮拜。
(C) 五百塊台幣。

問答 PART 2-6 問次數

Q1 Q: How often do they go to the museum?
(A) They usually go there.
(B) They often go to the museum.
(C) Once a week.

問題：他們多久去一次博物館？
(A) 他們經常去那裡。
(B) 他們通常去博物館。
(C) 一週一次。

Q2 Q: How often does she go to the library?
(A) Twice a week.
(B) It's at twelve o'clock.
(C) One more time.

問題：她多久去一次圖書館？
(A) 一週兩次。
(B) 它在十二點鐘的時候。
(C) 再一次。

問答 PART 2-7 問人的「身份」

Q1 Q: What is your mother?
(A) She is beautiful.
(B) She is a teacher.
(C) She is nice.

問題：你媽媽是做什麼的？
(A) 她很漂亮。
(B) 她是一位老師。
(C) 她人很好。

Q2 Q: You're Lisa's boyfriend, aren't you?
(A) Yes, I am.
(B) My name is Lily.
(C) How about you?

問題：你是莉莎的男朋友，不是嗎？
(A) 是的，我是。
(B) 我的名字叫莉莉。
(C) 你呢？

問答 PART 2-8 描述人的外表

Q1 Q: Who is the bald old man?
(A) He is Monica's grandpa.
(B) He is singing.
(C) I met him this morning.

問題：那個光頭的老先生是誰？
(A) 他是莫妮卡的爺爺。
(B) 他正在唱歌。
(C) 我今天早上遇到他。

Q2 Q: Who is the old woman?
(A) She is my grandmother.
(B) No, she is young.
(C) She is in the classroom.

問題：那位老太太是誰？
(A) 她是我外婆。
(B) 不，她很年輕。
(C) 她在教室裡。

A  

問答 PART 2-9 描述情緒與身體狀況

Q1 Q: I'm so nervous. I am the toastmaster of the banquet tonight.
(A) I love to eat toast.
(B) Take it easy. You can make it.
(C) You did a good job.

問題：我好緊張。我是今晚宴會的主持人。
(A) 我喜歡吃吐司。
(B) 放輕鬆。你可以做到的。
(C) 你做得很棒。

Q2 Q: I feel cold today.
(A) Would you like to have some hot tea?
(B) Let's go swimming.
(C) Take off your coat.

問題：今天我覺得冷。
(A) 你想要來點熱茶嗎？
(B) 我們去游泳吧。
(C) 脫掉你的外套。

問答 PART 2-10 表達個人喜好

Q1 Q: I love milk so much.
(A) So do I.
(B) Neither do I.
(C) Don't mention it.

問題：我好喜歡牛奶。
(A) 我也是。
(B) 我也不。
(C) 別客氣。

Q2 Q: What kind of food do you like?
(A) I like fish.
(B) I like zebra.
(C) I like kangaroo.

問題：你喜歡哪種食物？
(A) 我喜歡魚。
(B) 我喜歡斑馬。
(C) 我喜歡袋鼠。

問答 PART 2-11 問「嗜好」

Q1 Q: What do you often do in your free time?
(A) I'm not free tonight.
(B) Twice a week.
(C) See a movie.

問題：你有空時通常做些什麼？
(A) 我今晚沒有空。
(B) 一週兩次。
(C) 看電影。

Q2 Q: How did you play basketball so well?
(A) I played basketball with them yesterday.
(B) Let's play basketball.
(C) We practice playing basketball every day.

問題：你籃球怎麼打得這麼好？
(A) 我昨天和他們打籃球。
(B) 我們來打籃球吧。
(C) 我們每天練習打籃球。

問答 PART 2-12 描述「感受」

Q1 Q: How was the movie you saw yesterday?
(A) It's yummy.
(B) I saw the movie with Peter yesterday.
(C) It's so touching.

問題：你昨天看的那部電影如何？
(A) 它很美味。
(B) 我昨天和彼得去看電影。
(C) 它很感人。

Q2 Q: How was your winter vacation?
(A) That's too bad.
(B) From December 20th to January 5th.
(C) Great! I took a trip to Italy.

問題：你的寒假過得如何？
(A) 那太糟了。
(B) 從十二月二十日到一月五日。
(C) 很棒！我去義大利旅遊。

問答 PART 2-13 問「正在做什麼」

Q1 Q: Are they still playing video games upstairs?
(A) No, they are playing baseball outside.
(B) Yes, they're sleeping.
(C) No, I'm reading books.

問題：他們還在樓上打電動嗎？
(A) 不，他們在外面打棒球。
(B) 是的，他們在睡覺。
(C) 不，我正在讀書。

Q2 Q: Is Bill still having breakfast at home?
(A) No, he went to school five minutes ago.
(B) Yes, he's still sleeping at home.
(C) He had a sandwich.

問題：比爾還在家吃早餐嗎？
(A) 不，他五分鐘前去學校了。
(B) 是的，他還在家裡睡覺。
(C) 他吃了一個三明治。

問答 PART 2-14 問「將要做什麼」

Q1 Q: Will you do something special tomorrow?
(A) I'm still thinking about it.
(B) I went to the party.
(C) How nice it is!

問題：你明天要做什麼特別的事嗎？
(A) 我還在想。
(B) 我去了派對。
(C) 它多好啊！

Q2 Q: Will you go somewhere tomorrow morning?
(A) No, I'll go jogging.
(B) Yes, I'll go to the supermarket.
(C) Yes, I need to go.

問題：你明天早上要去哪裡嗎？
(A) 不，我要去慢跑。
(B) 是的，我要去超市。
(C) 是的，我需要去。

問答 PART 2-15 問「過去做了什麼」

Q1 Q: We went to the concert last night.
(A) How is the movie?
(B) What can I do for you?
(C) Did you enjoy it?

問題：我們昨晚去演唱會。
(A) 電影如何？
(B) 我能為你做什麼？
(C) 你喜歡嗎？

Q2 Q: Did you call me this afternoon?
(A) I'm talking on the phone.
(B) Yes, why didn't you come to school today?
(C) I don't have a cell phone.

A  

問題：你今天下午有打電話給我嗎？
(A) 我正在講電話。
(B) 是的，你今天怎麼沒來學校？
(C) 我沒有手機。

問答 PART 2-16 問「原因」

Q1 Q: Why didn't you go to school yesterday?
(A) I went to school by bus.
(B) I got a stomachache.
(C) I have no idea.

問題：你昨天為什麼沒有去學校？
(A) 我搭公車去學校。
(B) 我胃痛。
(C) 我不知道。

Q2 Q: Why didn't you have dinner?
(A) Have a good time!
(B) Thank you for coming.
(C) I decided to lose weight.

問題：為什麼你不吃晚餐？
(A) 玩得開心！
(B) 謝謝你來。
(C) 我決心要減重。

問答 PART 2-17 邀約

Q1 Q: Do you want a cup of coffee?
(A) It's hot today.
(B) Yes, please.
(C) I love beef.

問題：你想要來杯咖啡嗎？
(A) 今天很熱。
(B) 是的，麻煩你。
(C) 我喜歡牛肉。

Q2 Q: I made a pie. Do you want to try it?
(A) No, thanks. I'm full.
(B) That's all right.
(C) I don't have the time.

問題：我做了一個派。你想要吃看看嗎？
(A) 不，謝謝。我飽了。
(B) 沒關係。
(C) 我不知道現在幾點。

問答 PART 2-18 尋求建議與幫助

Q1 Q: Could you help me move those boxes?
(A) I have a good idea.
(B) Would you like to drink some water?
(C) No problem.

問題：你可以幫我搬那些箱子嗎？
(A) 我有個好主意。
(B) 你想要喝點水嗎？
(C) 沒問題。

Q2 Q: Can you help me this afternoon?
(A) Sure. What can I do?
(B) I will help you tomorrow.
(C) I can speak English well.

問題：你今天下午可以幫我嗎？
(A) 當然。我能做什麼？
(B) 我明天會幫你。
(C) 我英文說得好。

問答 PART 2-19 詢問「是否可以」

Q1 Q: Do you mind opening the window? 問題：你介意把窗戶打開嗎？

(A) Of course not. (A) 當然不介意。

(B) I have no idea. (B) 我不知道。

(C) This is mine. (C) 這是我的。

Q2 Q: Can I borrow your backpack? 問題：我可以借你的背包嗎？

(A) Don't worry. (A) 別擔心。

(B) Sure. Here you are. (B) 當然。拿去。

(C) I see. (C) 我知道了。

問答 PART 2-20 表達位置

Q1 Q: Where is the post office nearby? 問題：最近的郵局在哪裡？

(A) You can go there by bus 212. (A) 你可以搭 212 公車去那裡。

(B) Just walk straight, and turn left. (B) 直走，然後左轉。

(C) It's two hundred meters. (C) 它有兩百公尺遠。

Q2 Q: Where is the hospital? 問題：醫院在哪裡？

(A) It's in the sky. (A) 它在天空中。

(B) It's at the corner. (B) 它在轉角。

(C) You can take the bus. (C) 你可以搭公車。

問答 PART 2-21 詢問交通方式與距離

Q1 Q: How did you come to our villa? 問題：你怎麼來我們別墅的？

(A) Two hours. (A) 兩個小時。

(B) By taxi. (B) 搭計程車。

(C) Three million dollars. (C) 三百萬。

Q2 Q: How far is it from the park to the school? 問題：從公園到學校距離有多遠？

(A) Around 5 miles. (A) 大概五英哩。

(B) In twenty minutes. (B) 二十分鐘內。

(C) It's close to the station. (C) 它靠近車站。

問答 PART 2-22 問「何時」

Q1 Q: When is the TV program?
(A) It's at seven thirty.
(B) I also love it.
(C) Let's watch TV!

問題：那個電視節目是在何時？
(A) 它是在七點三十分。
(B) 我也很喜歡。
(C) 我們來看電視吧！

Q2 Q: What day is today?
(A) It's February.
(B) It's my birthday.
(C) It's Saturday.

問題：今天星期幾？
(A) 是二月。
(B) 是我的生日。
(C) 是星期六。

問答 PART 2-23 問「要多久時間」

Q1 Q: How much time do you need to eat a pizza?
(A) Five hundred NT dollars.
(B) I am so excited.
(C) Around twenty minutes.

問題：吃一個披薩你要花多久時間？
(A) 五百塊錢。
(B) 我好興奮。
(C) 大概二十分鐘。

Q2 Q: How long will Judy stay in London?
(A) In ten minutes.
(B) Tomorrow morning.
(C) About two weeks.

問題：茱蒂會在倫敦待多久？
(A) 在十分鐘內。
(B) 明天早上。
(C) 大約兩週。

問答 PART 2-24 肯定附和回答

Q1 Q: This is where I live.
(A) I live in Taipei.
(B) It looks comfortable.
(C) Do you like leaves?

問題：這就是我住的地方。
(A) 我住在台北。
(B) 它看起來很舒適。
(C) 你喜歡樹葉嗎？

Q2 Q: Halloween is coming.
(A) I will come.
(B) Yeah! I can't wait.
(C) Sorry. I can't come.

問題：萬聖節要來了。
(A) 我會來。
(B) 是啊！我等不及了。
(C) 抱歉。我不能來。

問答 PART 2-25 否定附和回答

Q1 Q: I can't go to your party because my mother is ill.
(A) That's great.
(B) It's a good idea.
(C) I'm sorry to hear that.

問題：我不能去你的派對，因為我媽媽生病了。
(A) 那很棒。
(B) 那是個好主意。
(C) 我很遺憾聽到這事。

Q2 Q: I can't believe you lied to me.
(A) You are a kind man.
(B) I'm terribly sorry.
(C) I wasn't lying on the bed then.

問題：我不敢相信你對我說謊。
(A) 你是個好心的人。
(B) 我真的很抱歉。
(C) 我那時沒有躺在床上。

YOUR TURN! 實力挑戰題

1 Q: What is the man?
(A) He is my father.
(B) He is handsome.
(C) He is a soldier.

問題：這個男人是做什麼的？
(A) 他是我爸爸。
(B) 他很帥。
(C) 他是一位士兵。

2 Q: How did you get that toy car?
(A) It's one hundred NT dollars.
(B) My dad bought it for me yesterday.
(C) It is cool, isn't it?

問題：你是如何得到這台玩具車的？
(A) 它要一百元。
(B) 我爸爸昨天買給我的。
(C) 它很酷，不是嗎？

3 Q: It's too bitter to drink.
(A) Is it good to drink?
(B) Do you need some sugar?
(C) It's really hot.

問題：它太苦了沒辦法喝。
(A) 它好喝嗎？
(B) 你需要一些糖嗎？
(C) 它很燙。

4 Q: When will the last train to Tainan leave?
(A) He comes here by train.
(B) It is coming.
(C) At eleven thirty.

問題：最後一班去台南的火車幾點離開？
(A) 他搭火車來這裡。
(B) 它來了。
(C) 在十一點三十分。

5 Q: How's the dish?
(A) It's delicious.
(B) He is fine.
(C) It's on the table.

問題：這道菜如何？
(A) 它很美味。
(B) 他很好。
(C) 它在餐桌上。

6 Q: Where are you going?
(A) We are cooks.
(B) I am her sister.
(C) We are going to the park.

問題：你要去哪裡？
(A) 我們是廚師。
(B) 我是她妹妹。
(C) 我們要去公園。

7 Q: Who is the lady with long blond hair?
(A) She's really pretty.
(B) She's sitting there.
(C) She is my cousin, Linda.

問題：那位有一頭金色長髮的女士是誰？
(A) 她真的很漂亮。
(B) 她就坐在那裡。
(C) 她是我表妹，琳達。

8 Q: Could you please pass me the salt?
(A) It's really salty.
(B) OK. Here you are.
(C) Sorry, I don't have it.

問題：你可以把鹽傳給我嗎？
(A) 它真的很鹹。
(B) 好的。給你。
(C) 抱歉。我沒有。

9 Q: How often do you go to that restaurant?
(A) I went there last night.
(B) Twice a week.
(C) It tastes good.

問題：你多久去一次那間餐廳？
(A) 我昨晚去了那裡。
(B) 一週兩次。
(C) 它嚐起來很好。

10 Q: Give me a call when you get home.
(A) OK, I will.
(B) I have no cell phone.
(C) I am talking on the phone.

問題：你到家時給我個電話。
(A) 好的，我會的。
(B) 我沒有手機。
(C) 我正在講電話。

簡短對話 PART 3-1 問「說話者在說什麼」

Q1

W: Look, there is a puppy sleeping on the road.
M: It's really dangerous. Where is its owner?
W: Maybe it's a stray dog.
M: Let's go to help it.
Q: What are the speakers talking about?
(A) A dog.
(B) A child.
(C) A road.

女：看，有隻小狗正在馬路上睡覺。
男：那真危險。牠的主人在哪裡？
女：也許牠是隻流浪狗。
男：我們去幫牠吧。
問題：說話者在談論些什麼？
(A) 一隻狗。
(B) 一個小孩。
(C) 一條馬路。

Q2

M: How was your trip to Greece?
F : Oh, it's great. Greece is really a beautiful place.
M: Really? I am planning to go there this summer.
F : You must go there.
Q: Which place are they talking about?
(A) Honeymoon
(B) Greece
(C) America

男：你的希臘之旅如何？
女：哦，很棒。希臘真的是個很美的地方。
男：真的嗎？我正計劃今年暑假要去那裡。
女：你一定要去看看。
問題：他們在談論哪個地方？
(A) 蜜月
(B) 希臘
(C) 美國

簡短對話 PART 3-2 問說話者正在做什麼

Q1

M: Happy birthday!
F: Wow! Thank you for the gifts and the cake.
M: Make a wish!
F: I wish my family and friends all happiness.
Q: What are the speakers doing?
(A) Celebrating a birthday
(B) Making a birthday cake
(C) Buying birthday gifts

男：生日快樂！
女：哇！謝謝你的禮物和蛋糕。
男：許個願！
女：我希望我的家人和朋友們都幸福。
問題：說話者在做什麼？
(A) 慶祝生日。
(B) 做一個生日蛋糕。
(C) 買生日禮物。

Q2

W: May I help you?
M: Yes, I want four cups of coffee to go.
W: OK. Ice or hot?
M: Three hot coffee and one ice coffee.
Q: What is the man doing?
(A) Drinking coffee.
(B) Buying coffee.
(C) Making coffee.

女：我能為您服務嗎？
男：是的，我要外帶四杯咖啡。
女：好的。冰的還是熱的？
男：三杯熱咖啡和一杯冰咖啡。
問題：這個男人正在做什麼？
(A) 喝咖啡。
(B) 買咖啡。
(C) 泡咖啡。

簡短對話 PART 3-3 問說話者想要、將要做什麼

Q1 M: Why don't you go to Anna's birthday?
F : I will, but I don't want to let her know now.
M: Oh, I see. You want to give her a surprise.
F : That's right. Please don't tell her.
Q: Will the woman go to Anna's birthday?
(A) Yes, she will.
(B) No, she won't.
(C) She will give her a surprise.

男：為什麼你不去參加安娜的生日？
女：我會去，但我現在不想讓她知道。
男：哦，我懂了。你想要給她一個驚喜。
女：沒錯。請不要告訴她。
問題：這個女人會去參加安娜的生日嗎？
(A) 是的，她會。
(B) 不，她不會。
(C) 她會給她一個驚喜。

Q2 M: Mom, I want to buy a new bike.
F : You have a bike already.
M: But I want to have a new one.
F : No way.
Q: What will the mother do?
(A) She will buy a new bike for her son.
(B) She will find the way.
(C) She won't buy a new bike for her son.

男：媽媽，我想要買一輛新的腳踏車。
女：你已經有一輛腳踏車了。
男：但我想要一輛新的。
女：不行。
問題：這個媽媽會做什麼？
(A) 她會買一輛新腳踏車給他兒子。
(B) 她會找到那條路的。
(C) 她不會幫她兒子買一輛新腳踏車。

簡短對話 PART 3-4 問說話者本身的訊息

Q1 M: Are you ready to order now?
F : Yes, we would like to have two pieces of cheese cake.
M: Sorry, we don't have cheese cake now. Would you like to have chocolate cake?
F : OK, two pieces of chocolate cake, please.
Q: What is the man?
(A) He is a baker.
(B) He is a waiter.
(C) He is a cook.

男：你們準備好要點餐了嗎？
女：是的，我們想要兩片起司蛋糕。
男：抱歉，我們現在沒有起司蛋糕。你們想要巧克力蛋糕嗎？
女：好吧，請給我們兩片巧克力蛋糕。
問題：這個男人是做什麼的？
(A) 他是一位烘焙師。
(B) 他是一位服務生。
(C) 他是一位廚師。

Q2 W: Excuse me, sir. Is the bus going to Taipei Station?
M: Yes, get on the bus.
W: How much is the ticket?
M: It's fifteen dollars.
Q: What is the man?
(A) He's a taxi driver.
(B) He's a bus driver.
(C) He's a clerk.

女：先生，請問一下。這輛公車有去台北車站嗎？
男：是的，上車吧。
女：票價是多少錢？
男：十五塊錢。
問題：這個男人是做什麼的？
(A) 是一位計程車司機。
(B) 他是一位公車司機。
(C) 他是一位店員。

簡短對話 PART 3-5 問說話者在哪裡

Q1 W: May I help you?
M: I want two pizzas and a bottle of coke.
W: OK. Please wait a minute. Do you have a VIP card?
M: Yes, here you are.
Q: Where are the speakers?
(A) In a pizza parlor.
(B) In a warehouse.
(C) In a grocery store.

女：我能幫您嗎？
男：我要兩個披薩和一瓶可樂。
女：好的。請等一下。你有 VIP 貴賓卡嗎？
男：有，給你。
問題：說話者在哪裡？
(A) 在一間披薩店。
(B) 在一間五金行。
(C) 在一間雜貨店。

Q2 F : Good morning, everyone. Who is absent today?
M: Miss Lin, Jack felt ill this morning, so he can't come today.
F: OK. Please tell him we have an exam tomorrow morning, so he has to come to school tomorrow. Let's open the book, and turn to page ten.
Q: Where are they?
(A) In the office.
(B) In the hospital.
(C) In the classroom.

女：大家早安。今天有誰缺席？
男：林老師，傑克今天早上覺得不舒服，所以他今天不能來。
女：好的。請跟他說我們明天早上要考試，所以他明天得來學校。我們打開書，翻到第十頁。
問題：他們在哪裡？
(A) 在辦公室。
(B) 在醫院。
(C) 在教室。

簡短對話 PART 3-6 問說話者要去哪裡

Q1

M: Where are you going?
F : I am going to the convenience store.
M: Could you buy me a cup of coffee?
F : Yes, I will be back soon.
Q: Where is the woman going?
(A) a coffee shop
(B) a convenience store
(C) a bookstore

男：你要去哪裡？
女：我要去便利商店。
男：你可以幫我買杯咖啡嗎？
女：好的，我馬上就回來。
問題：這個女生要去哪裡？
(A) 一間咖啡店。
(B) 一間便利商店。
(C) 一間書店。

Q2

M: Hey, I can give you a ride. Get in the car.
W: Are you sure? You just drink some beer.
M: That's OK. I'm still awake.
W: You shouldn't drink and drive. Let's take the bus home.
Q: How will the speakers go home?
(A) By the man's car.
(B) By bus.
(C) On foot.

男：嘿，我可以載你一程。上車吧。
女：你確定？你才喝了些啤酒。
男：沒關係。我還是很清醒。
女：你不應該酒後開車。我們搭公車回家吧。
問題：說話者會如何回家？
(A) 搭這男人的車子。
(B) 搭公車。
(C) 走路。

簡短對話 PART 3-7 問「東西在哪裡」

Q1

M: Did you see my jacket?
W: Isn't it on the sofa?
M: No, it's not there.
W: I see it. It's under the sofa.
Q: Where is the jacket?
(A) Above the sofa.
(B) On the sofa.
(C) Under the sofa.

男：你有看到我的夾克嗎？
女：它不是在沙發上嗎？
男：不，它不在那。
女：我看到了。它在沙發底下。
問題：夾克在哪裡？
(A) 在沙發上方。
(B) 在沙發上。
(C) 在沙發底下。

Q2 B: Did you take my math textbook, Gina?
G: No. I just saw it on your desk. Did you put it in your bag?
B: No, I can't find it in my bag.
G: Hey, it's under your desk.
Q: Where is the math textbook?
(A) In the boy's bag.
(B) On the desk.
(C) Under the desk.

男：吉娜，你有拿我的數學課本嗎？
女：沒有，我剛才看到它在你的書桌上。你有把它放進袋子裡嗎？
男：沒有，袋子裡我沒找到。
女：嘿，它在你的書桌底下。
問題：數學課本在哪裡？
(A) 在這男孩的袋子裡。
(B) 在書桌上。
(C) 在書桌底下。

簡短對話 PART 3-8 問發生的事

Q1 F: How was your weekend?
M: I stayed at home on Saturday, and went fishing with friends on Sunday.
F: I also love fishing.
M: Maybe you can join us next time.
Q: How did the woman spend her weekend?
(A) Stayed at home
(B) Went fishing
(C) We don't know.

女：你週末過得如何？
男：我週六待在家裡，週日和朋友去釣魚。
女：我也喜歡釣魚。
男：也許你下次可以加入我們。
問題：這個女人如何度過週末？
(A) 待在家裡。
(B) 去釣魚。
(C) 我們不知道。

Q2 F: What are you doing?
M: I'm looking for my English book. I remember I put it in my bag last night.
F: Are you sure? Didn't you leave it on your desk?
M: Maybe you're right.
Q: What is the boy's problem?
(A) He forgot to bring the English book.
(B) He found the English book.
(C) He didn't carry his bag.

女：你在做什麼？
男：我正在找我的英文書。我記得我昨晚把它放在我的袋子裡。
女：你確定嗎？你不是把它留在你桌上了嗎
男：也許你是對的。
問題：這個男孩的問題是什麼？
(A) 他忘了帶英文書來。
(B) 他發現了該本英文書。
(C) 他沒有帶他的袋子。

簡短對話 PART 3-9 問說話者的想法

Q1 F: Do you like that kind of car?
M: Not really. The shape is ugly and I want a bigger one.
F: How much do you want to pay for a car?
M: About five hundred thousand dollars.
Q: Does the man like that kind of car?
(A) Yes, he likes it very much.
(B) No, he didn't have any money.
(C) No, he thinks the shape is ugly.

女：你喜歡那種車子嗎？
男：不。那外型太醜了，而且我想要大一點的。
女：你打算花多少錢買車？
男：大概五十萬。
問題：這個男人喜歡這種車嗎？
(A) 是的，他很喜歡。
(B) 不，他沒有錢。
(C) 不，他覺得那外型很醜。

Q2 F: Wow, cool! Is that your new jacket?
M: Yeah, I just bought it in the Shilin Night Market last night.
F: It looks nice. How much was it?
M: It's only $580.
Q: What does the woman think about the jacket?
(A) It's cheap.
(B) It's nice.
(C) It's expensive.

女：哇，酷！那是你的新夾克嗎？
男：是啊，我昨晚才在士林夜市買的。
女：它看起來很不錯。多少錢？
男：只要五百八十塊。
問題：這個女人覺得這件夾克如何？
(A) 它很便宜。
(B) 很不錯。
(C) 它很貴。

簡短對話 PART 3-10 原因類的題型

Q1 M: I'm sorry!
F : Why?
M: I broke your favorite cup.
F : Never mind.
Q: Why does the man say he is sorry to the woman?
(A) They are not good friends.
(B) He loves the cup.
(C) He broke the woman's favorite cup.

男：我很抱歉！
女：為什麼？
男：我弄破了你最喜愛的杯子。
女：別介意。
問題：為什麼這男人會對這女人說抱歉？
(A) 他們不是好朋友。
(B) 他喜歡那個杯子。
(C) 他弄破了那女人最喜愛的杯子。

Q2 F: Is Jack there?
M: Speaking.
F: Jack, I'm sorry. I'm not feeling well today, so I can't go to your party tonight.
M: That's all right! Get more rest!
Q: Why doesn't the woman go to Jack's party?
(A) She can't catch the bus.
(B) She is speaking.
(C) She is sick.

女：傑克在嗎？
男：我就是。
女：傑克，我很抱歉。我今天覺得不舒服，所以我今晚不能去參加你的派對了。
男：沒關係。多休息吧！
問題：為什麼這女人不去傑克的派對？
(A) 她不能趕上公車。
(B) 她正在說話。
(C) 她生病了。

簡短對話 PART 3-11 和時間有關的對話

Q1 M: Hey, how about riding a bike with me tomorrow morning?
W: I don't want to wake up early. Can we ride a bike tomorrow evening?
M: OK, see you tomorrow.
Q: When will the speakers ride the bike?
(A) Tomorrow morning.
(B) Tomorrow afternoon.
(C) Tomorrow evening.

男：嘿，明天早上要不要和我一起去騎腳踏車？
女：我不想要早起。我們可以明天傍晚去騎車嗎？
男：好的，明天見。
問題：說話者何時會去騎腳踏車？
(A) 明天上午。
(B) 明天下午。
(C) 明天傍晚。

Q2 W: Tom, where did you go last night?
M: I stayed at home and watched TV.
W: Are you sure? I called you last night, but no one answered the phone.
M: When did you call?
W: Around nine.
M: I was taking a bath then.
Q: When was the man taking a bath last night?
(A) At nine.
(B) At eight.
(C) At seven.

女：湯姆，你昨晚去哪裡了？
男：我待在家裡看電視。
女：你確定？我昨晚打電話給你，但沒人接電話。
男：你幾點打來的？
女：大概九點。
男：我那時正在洗澡。
問題：這個男人昨晚何時洗澡？
(A) 九點。
(B) 八點。
(C) 七點。

簡短對話 PART 3-12 和數字有關的對話

Q1 M: This is my new jacket.
F : It is cool. How much is it?
M: It is only 250 dollars.
F : Wow, it's so cheap.
Q: How much is the jacket?
(A) 350 dollars
(B) 250 dollars
(C) 150 dollars

男：這是我的夾克。
女：它很酷。多少錢？
男：它只要兩百五十元。
女：哇，它好便宜。
問題：這件夾克多少錢？
(A) 350 元。
(B) 250 元。
(C) 150 元。

Q2 M: What is your cell phone number?
F : It's zero nine two three, zero two five, zero one four.(0923-025-014)
M: Is it zero nine two three, zero five two, zero four one? (0923-052-041)
F : No, it's zero nine two three, zero two five, zero one four. (0923-025-014)
Q: What is the woman's cell phone number?
(A) 0923-052-041
(B) 0923-025-014
(C) 0923-052-014

男：你的手機號碼幾號？
女：0923-025-014。
男：是 0923-052-041 嗎？
女；不，是 0923-025-014。
問題：這個女人的手機號碼是幾號？
(A) 0923-052-041
(B) 0923-025-014
(C) 0923-052-014

簡短對話 PART 3-13 問「對與錯」

Q1 M: I am going to America next year.
F : How long will you stay there?
M: I will stay there for two years.
F : It's a long time. I will miss you very much.
Q: Which one is NOT true about the man?
(A) He is going to America tomorrow.
(B) He will go to America next year.
(C) He will stay in America for two years.

男：我明年要去美國。
女：你要在那待多久？
男：我會待在那兩年。
女：好長的時間。我會很想念你的。
問題：關於這個男的何者不是真的？
(A) 他明天要去美國了。
(B) 他明年會去美國。
(C) 他會在美國待兩年。

Q2 M: Do you speak English?
F : Yes, do you need some help?
M: Could you tell me where the Taipei 101 is?
F : You are just in front of it.
Q: Which one is NOT true?
(A) The man is in front of the Taipei 101.
(B) The woman doesn't speak English.
(C) The woman is glad to help the man.

男：你會說英文嗎？
女：會，你需要幫忙嗎？
男：你可以告訴我台北 101 在哪裡嗎？
女：你就在它的正前方。
問題：哪一個不是真的？
(A) 這個男人正在台北 101 的前方。
(B) 這個女人不會說英文。
(C) 這個女人很樂意幫助這個男人。

A  C

YOUR TURN! 實力挑戰題

1 F: My boss made me work on Sunday.
M: That sounds like a hard project.
F: Yeah, it is. He told me to finish the work. We stayed at the office until midnight.
M: That's terrible.
Q: What did the woman's boss do?
(A) The boss made the woman go home.
(B) The boss made the woman work on Sunday.
(C) The woman made the boss work with her on Sunday.

女：我老闆要我週日上班。
男：聽起來是個很困難的計劃。
女：是，它是。他要我完成這項工作。我們一直在辦公室待到半夜。
男：太慘了。
問題：這女人的老闆做了什麼？
(A) 這個老闆要那女人回家。
(B) 這個老闆要這女人週日上班。
(C) 這個女人要老闆週日和她一起上

A  

2 M: Surprise!
F : What?
M: Today is our anniversary. Don't you remember that?
F : Oh, I forgot it. Sorry, honey.
Q: Why did the woman say sorry to the man?
(A) She forgot his birthday.
(B) She forgot their anniversary.
(C) She didn't remember the surprise.

男：大驚喜！
女：什麼？
男：今天是我們的週年紀念。你不記得了嗎
女：噢，我忘了。抱歉，親愛的。
問題：為什麼這個女人要對男人說抱歉？
(A) 她忘了他的生日。
(B) 她忘了他們的週年紀念。
(C) 她不記得這個驚喜。

A  

3 M: Are you Mandy?
W: Yes, you are…?
M: I'm Gina's brother. My name is Bill.
W: Oh, good to see you, Bill.
Q: Which one is true?
(A) Bill is Gina's brother.
(B) Bill is Mandy's brother.
(C) Gina is Bill's friend.

男：你是曼蒂嗎？
女：是的，你是…？
男：我是吉娜的哥哥。我的名字是比爾。
女：噢，很高興見到你，比爾。
問題：哪一個是真的？
(A) 比爾是吉娜的哥哥。
(B) 比爾是曼蒂的哥哥。
(C) 吉娜是比爾的朋友。

4 F: Tom, turn off the TV and go to bed. It's late.
M: Mom, I'm not sleepy. I will go to bed later.
F: It's eleven thirty. Go to bed right away.
M: Mom, please…. Just five more minutes. The basketball game will come to an end soon.
Q: Why doesn't Tom want to go to bed?
(A) He is turning off the TV.
(B) He is playing basketball.
(C) He is watching a basketball game on TV.

女：湯姆，電視關掉然後去睡覺。太晚了。
男：媽，我還不睏。我等一下會去睡。
女：已經十一點三十分。現在就上床睡覺。
男：媽，拜託…再五鐘就好。這場籃球賽馬上就要結束了。
問題：為什麼湯姆不想上床睡覺？
(A) 他正在關掉電視。
(B) 他正在打籃球。
(C) 他正在看電視上的籃球比賽。

5 M: Excuse me. Do you know how I can get to Ruby restaurant?
W: There's no bus stop near that restaurant, so you have to take a taxi to get there.
M: Thank you for your help.
Q: How will the man go to Ruby restaurant?
(A) By bus.
(B) By train.
(C) By taxi.

男：抱歉。你知道我能怎麼去露比餐廳嗎？
女：餐廳附近沒有公車站牌，所以你得搭計程車去那裡。
男：謝謝你的幫忙。
題：這男人要如何去露比餐廳？
(A) 搭公車。
(B) 搭火車。
(C) 搭計程車。

6 M: What did you do last night?
F: I studied all night.
M: But I heard someone singing in your room.
F: Oh, I like to study with my radio on.
Q: What did the girl do last night?
(A) The girl went to a movie.
(B) She turned on the radio when she studied.
(C) She turned off the radio when she studied.

男：你昨晚做了什麼？
女：我整晚用功讀書。
男：但我聽到有人在你房間唱歌。
女：噢，我喜歡一邊讀書一邊開著收音機。
問題：那女孩昨晚做了什麼？
(A) 那女孩去看電影。
(B) 她讀書時把收音機開著。
(C) 她讀書時把收音機關掉。

Ⓐ  

7 M: May I take your order now?
W: Yes, we want two beefsteaks.
M: Would you like to drink anything?
W: Well, a cup of black tea and a glass of orange juice.
M: OK, please wait a moment.
Q: Where is the conversation taking place?
(A) In the toy store.
(B) In the flower shop.
(C) In the restaurant.

男：我可以幫你們點餐了嗎？
女：是的，我們想要兩客牛排。
男：你們想要喝點什麼嗎？
女：嗯，一杯紅茶和一杯柳橙汁。
男：好的，請稍待一下。
問題：這段對話發生在哪裡？
(A) 在玩具店。
(B) 在花店。
(C) 在餐廳。

Ⓐ  

8 W: Are you going to the library later?
M: Yes, I'm going there to write the report.
W: Could you just help me return these books?
M: OK, no problem.
Q: What is the man going to do?
(A) Go to the library.
(B) Buy some books.
(C) Watch TV.

女：你等一下要去圖書館嗎？
男：是的，我要去那裡寫報告。
女：你能幫我歸還這些書嗎？
男：好的，沒問題。
問題：這個男人要去做什麼？
(A) 去圖書館。
(B) 買一些書。
(C) 看電視。

Ⓐ  Ⓒ

9

M: This is a ticket of a piano concert.
F : Wow, there is your name on it. Are you going to have your piano concert?
M: Yes, I am so excited, but also a little worried.
F : I believe you can do it well. Good luck.
Q: Why is the man worried?
(A) He is too excited.
(B) He is going to have his piano concert.
(C) He is going to the piano concert.

男：這是鋼琴演奏會的票。
女：哇，上面有你的名字耶。你要有自己的鋼琴演奏會了嗎？
男：是的，我很興奮，但又有點擔心。
女：我相信你一定能表現很好。祝好運。
問題：為什麼這個男人擔心？
(A) 他太興奮了。
(B) 他要有自己的鋼琴演奏會了。
(C) 他要去鋼琴演奏會。

10

M: Do you want to go to a movie with me?
F : I want to go with you, but I can't.
M: Why?
F : I have to study English.
Q: Will the woman see a movie with the man?
(A) Yes, she will.
(B) No, she won't
(C) Yes, she won't.

男：你想要跟我去看電影嗎？
女：我想要跟你去，但我不行。
男：為什麼？
女：我得唸英文。
問題：這個女人會和這男人去看電影嗎？
(A) 是的，她會。
(B) 不，她不會。
(C) 是的，她不會。

短文聽解 PART 4-1 公開廣播類

Q1 Please look at the following three pictures.

Listen to the following announcement. Where will you most probably hear this announcement?

Thank you for taking Happy Bus. When you are on the bus, please lower your voice. Th priority seats are for the elderly, pregnant women, disabled passengers, children an passengers with babies. Smoking and eating are not allowed on the bus. Thank you for you cooperation.

請看以下的三張圖片。

注意聽接下來的廣播。你最有可能在哪裡聽到這段廣播？

謝謝您搭乘快樂巴士。當您在公車上時，請降低您的音量。博愛座是給長輩、懷孕婦女及行動不便者、孩童及帶嬰孩的乘客使用。車上禁止吸煙及飲食。謝謝您的合作。

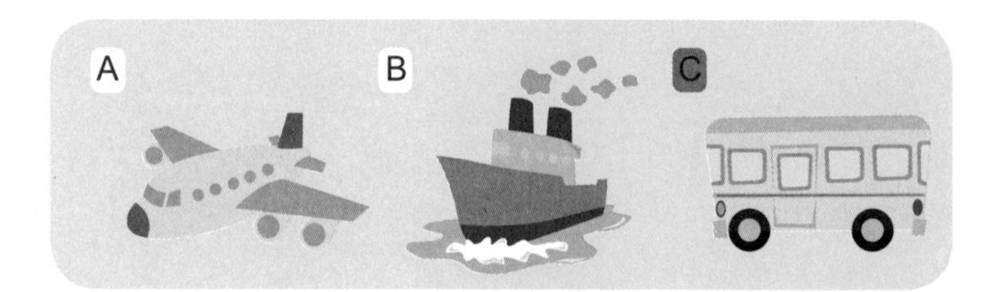

Q2 Please look at the following three pictures.

Listen to the following announcement. Which place suits the description best?

Welcome to the National Dr. Sun Yat-sen Memorial Hall. Please keep your voice down and turn off your mobile phone. Video taping and eating are not allowed here. If you need any help please come to our information desk. It is near the entrance. We will be glad to help you.

請看以下的三張圖片。

注意聽接下來的廣播。哪個地方最符合描述的內容？

歡迎來到國父紀念館。請降低您的音量並關掉您的手機。這裡禁止錄影及飲食。若您需要任何協助，請到我們的服務台。它就在入口的附近。我們會很高興為您服務。

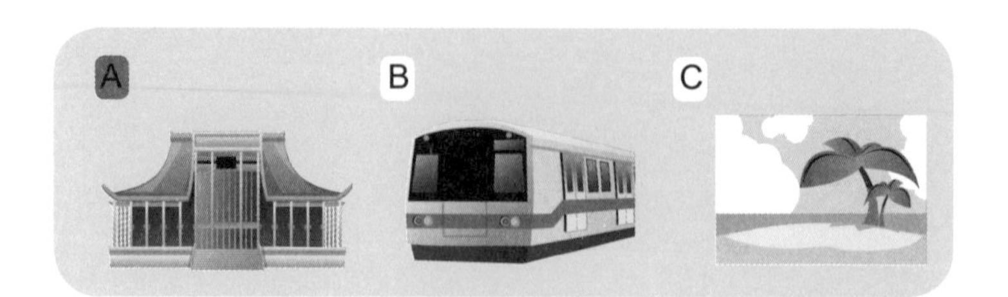

短文聽解 PART 4-2 留言類

Q1 Please look at the following three pictures.
Listen to the following message for Linda. What will Emily probably do tomorrow?
Linda, this is Emily. Are you going out for dinner? I will go hiking tomorrow morning. Would you like to come with me? Maybe we can have breakfast first, and then go hiking. Call me back soon.
請看以下的三張圖片。
注意聽給琳達的留言。艾蜜莉明天有可能會做什麼？
琳達，我是艾蜜莉。你出去吃晚飯了嗎？我明天早上會去登山健行。你要跟我一起去嗎？也許我們可以先吃早餐，然後去登山健行。趕快回電話給我。

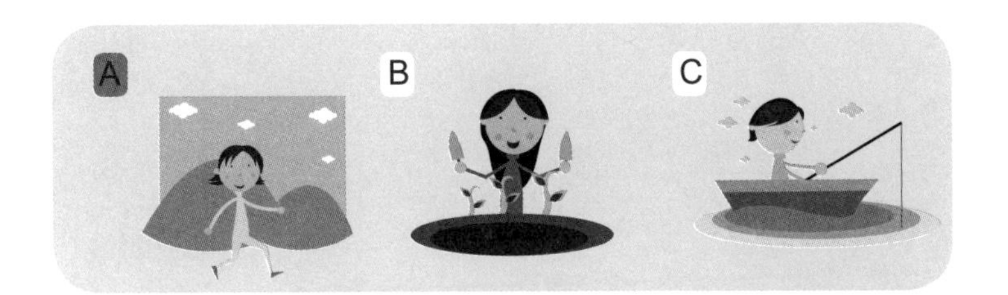

Q2 Please look at the following three pictures.
Tim left a message on Jennifer's answering machine. Where will Jennifer and Frank probably go tomorrow?
Hi, Jennifer. This is Tim. I want to tell you that I can't go camping with you and Frank tomorrow. I already have a date with my friends. I hope you and Frank will have a good time tomorrow. Bye!
請看以下的三張圖片。
提姆在珍妮佛的答錄機裡留了一則訊息。珍妮佛和法蘭克明天有可能會去哪裡？
嗨，珍妮佛。我是提姆。我想要跟你說我明天沒辦法和你和法蘭克去露營了。我已經和我的朋友有約了。我希望你和法蘭克明天玩得愉快。再見！

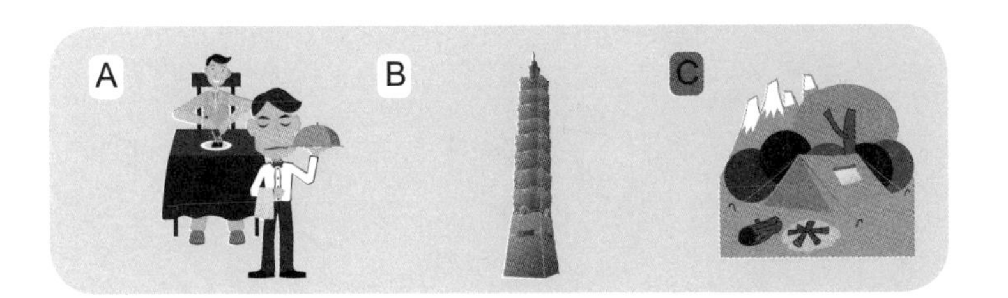

短文聽解 PART 4-3 新聞、氣象播報類

Q1 Please look at the following three pictures.
Listen to an announcement from the city government on TV. What does this announcement as
people to do?
Whether you ride a scooter or drive a car, remember to have respect for others on the roac
Follow the traffic rules, even if you see that many others do not follow them. If more and mor
people don't pay attention to any of the rules, no one will feel safe on city streets. The polic
can't solve all the problems, so please do your part.
請看以下的三張圖片。
注意聽這段政府在電視上的宣導。這則宣導要人們做什麼？
不論你是否騎摩托車或開車，請記得要尊重馬路上的其他人。就算你看到許多其他人沒有遵守交
通規則，請你還是要遵守。若愈來愈多人不注意交通規則，在城市的街道上沒有人會覺得有安全
感。警力無法解決所有的問題，所以請您盡您的本份。

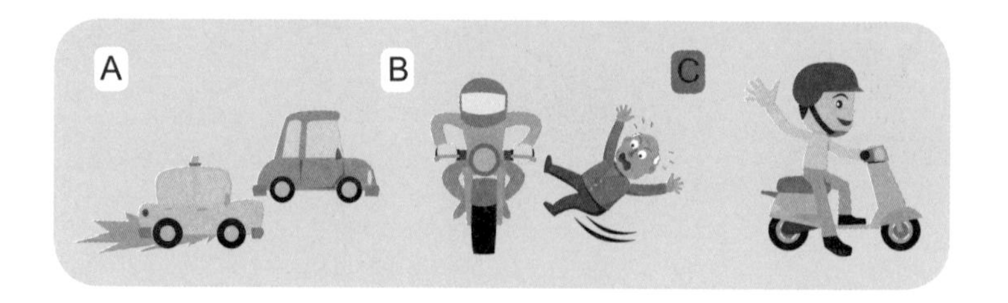

Q2 Please look at the following three pictures.
Listen to the following weather forecast. Benson will go to Taipei on Saturday. What does he
have to take with him?
The Central Weather Bureau has issued a cold weather warning. From Friday to Sunday, the
temperature will be under 10 degree Celsius especially in Northern Taiwan. The cold weather
will last until next week.
請看以下的三張圖片。
注意聽接下來的氣象預報。班生星期六會去台北。他得要帶什麼在身上？
中央氣象局發布低溫特報。從週五至週日，氣溫會降到攝氏十度以下，尤其是在北台灣地區。冷
天將持續到下週。

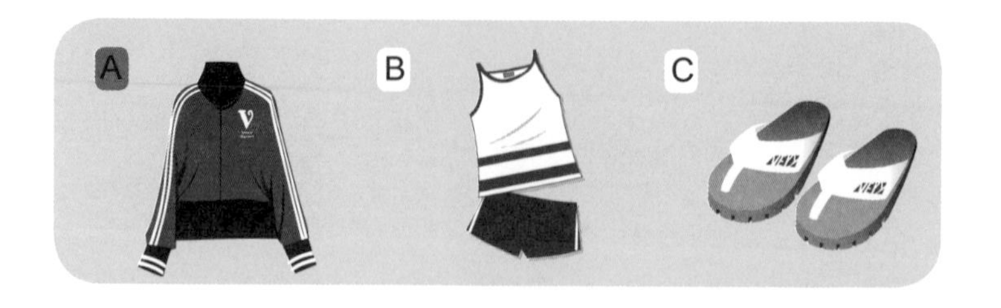

短文聽解 PART 4-4 人、事、物描述類

Q1 Please look at the following three pictures.
Listen to the following short talk. Which one is Vicky?
My friend, Vicky, is a ten-year-old girl. She has short blond hair and smiles all the time. She usually wears a purple dress and carries a red handbag when she goes out. Her dream is to be an excellent model in the future.
請看以下的三張圖片。
注意聽接下來的短文。哪一個是維琪？
我的朋友，維琪，是一位十歲的女孩。她有一頭金色短髮，也總是有笑臉。她通常穿著紫色的洋裝，出門時帶著一個紅色手提包。她的夢想是未來要成為一位優秀的模特兒。

Q2 Please look at the following three pictures.
Listen to the following short talk. What can we find in Healthy Shoes Shop?
Healthy Shoes Shop is located at Happy Street. They sell all kinds of shoes for women. It is open from 10:30 a.m. to 11:00 p.m. every day. From November 25 to December 31, they are giving a special discount of 20% on all boots.
請看以下的三張圖片。
注意聽接下來的短文。我們在健康鞋店可以找到什麼？
健康鞋店位於快樂街。他們賣各式各樣的女鞋。它的營業時間是每天早上十點半到晚上十一點。自十一月二十五日到十二月三十一日，他們所有的靴子都會有八折的特別折扣。

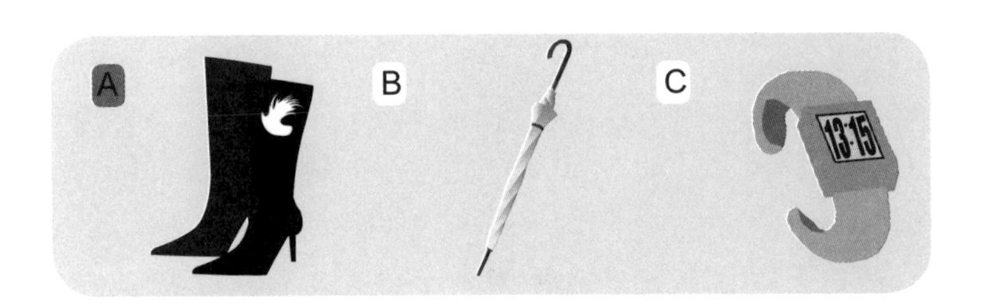

YOUR TURN! 實力挑戰題

1 Please look at the following three pictures.
What is mentioned in the following short talk?
Alice loves flowers so much. There is a beautiful garden at the back of her house. She plante
a lot of flowers, such as roses, sunflowers, daisies and tulips. Her favorite flower is th
sunflower. It looks just like the sun.
請看以下的三張圖片。
在以下的短文中提到的是哪一個？
艾莉絲很喜歡花。她家的後方有一個很漂亮的花園。她種了很多花，像是玫瑰、向日葵、小雛菊
和鬱金香。她最喜歡的花是向日葵。它看起來就像太陽一樣。

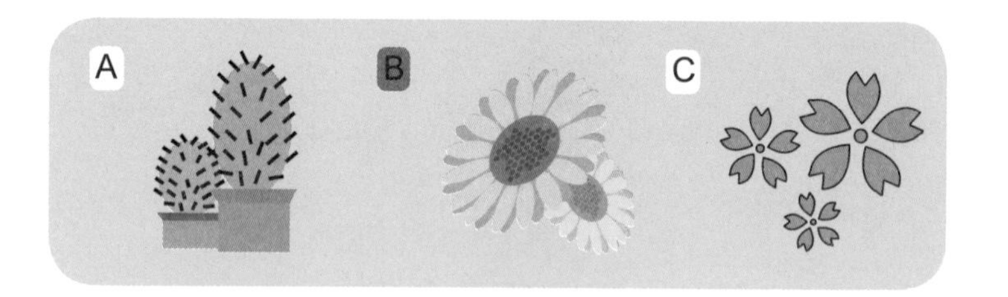

2 Please look at the following three pictures.
Listen to the following announcement. Which place suits the description best?
Good evening, ladies and gentlemen. Welcome to Steven's Magic Show. My name is Steven
Magic. You can call me Steven or Mr. Magic. I'm happy to meet all of you here. Now, I need a
partner to help me. Any volunteers? Please raise your hand.
請看以下的三張圖片。
注意聽接下來的廣播。哪一個地方最符合描述的內容？
各位先生女士晚安。歡迎來的史蒂芬的魔術秀。我的名字叫史蒂芬魔術。你可以叫我史蒂芬或魔
術先生。我很高興在這裡見到你們。現在，我需要一個夥伴來幫我。有志願者嗎？請舉手。

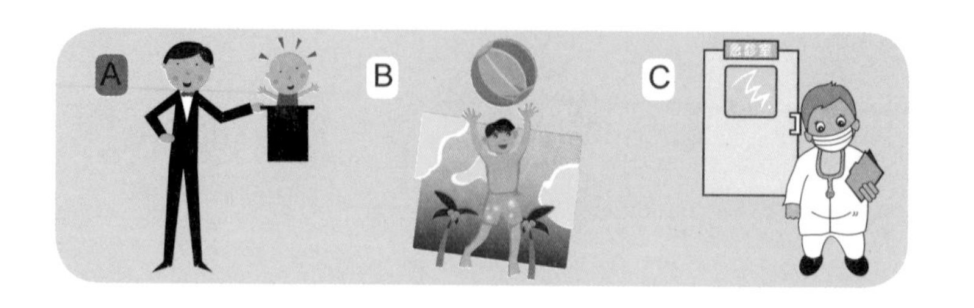

3 Please look at the following three pictures.
Bill left a message on Tony's answering machine. What will Bill do tomorrow afternoon?
Hi, Tony, this is Bill. Are you not at home? I want to tell you that I can't go swimming with you tomorrow afternoon. My grandma and grandpa will visit me tomorrow, and we will have lunch together. Sorry! Bye!
請看以下的三張圖片。
比爾在湯尼的答錄機上留了一則留言。比爾明天下午會做什麼？
嗨，湯尼，我是比爾。你不在家嗎？我要跟你說我明天下午沒辦法跟你去游泳了。我外婆和外公明天要來拜訪我，我們要一起吃午餐。抱歉！再見！

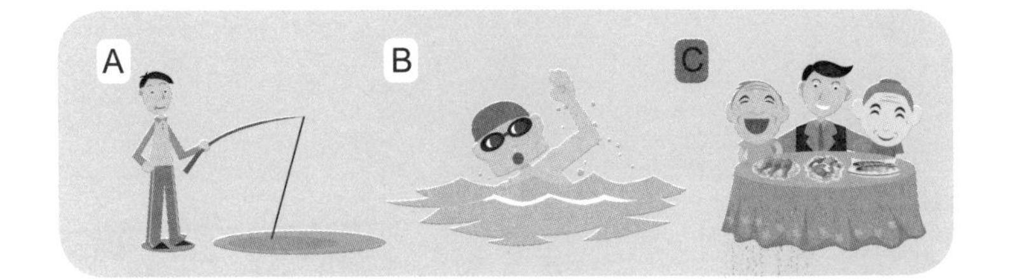

4 Please look at the following three pictures.
Listen to the following announcement. Where would you probably hear it?
Attention all passengers. Please be sure to keep your bag with you at all times. If any bags are found sitting around, we will take them. Also, please be sure you have your passport and boarding pass ready when it is time to get on board. Anyone without a boarding pass will not be allowed to board the flight.
請看以下的三張圖片。
注意聽以下的廣播。你有可能在哪裡聽到它？
各位乘客請注意。請隨時確認您的袋子有在您身邊。若發現有任何無人在旁的袋子，我們會將它們拿走。同時，請在登機時確認您有攜帶護照及登機證。沒有攜帶登機證的人將無法登機。

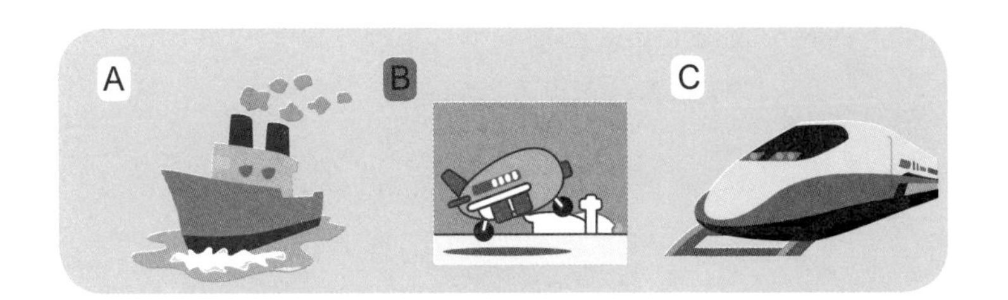

5 Please look at the following three pictures.
What is mentioned in the following short talk?
Benson spent a lot of money yesterday. He treated his girlfriend to lunch. It cost him NT$1
After lunch, they went to Happy Department Store. He bought a pair of high heels for his girlf
and a pair of sun glasses for himself. They cost him NT$ 3600. He almost ran out of all c
salary this month.
請看以下的三張圖片。
以下的短文中提到了哪一個？
班生昨天花了很多錢。他請她的女友吃午餐。那花了他一千兩百元。午餐之後，他們去了快樂
公司。他買了一雙高跟鞋給她的女朋友，還給自己買了一副太陽眼鏡。它們花了他三千六百元
幾乎要花光了他這個月的所有薪水。

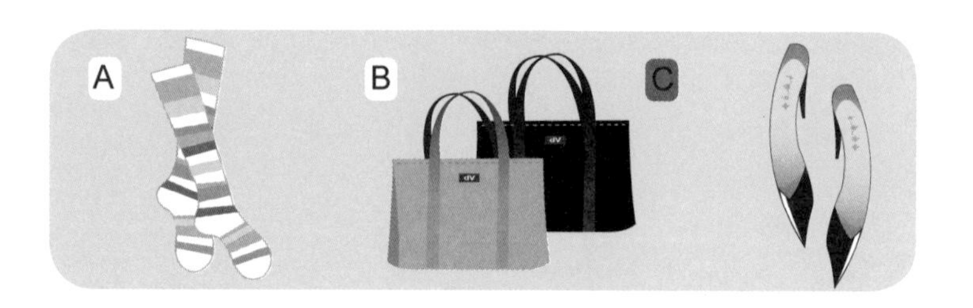

學習成果測驗 PART 1 看圖辨義

Q1

Ⓐ Ⓑ Ⓒ

Q: Where is the little boy?
(A) He's standing next to the man.
(B) He's standing behind the man.
(C) He's sitting in front of the man.
問題：這個小男孩在哪裡？
(A) 他正站在這男人的旁邊。
(B) 他正站在這男人的後面。
(C) 他正坐在這男人的前面。

Q2

Q: How does the man feel?

(A) He feels sleepy.

(B) He feels excited.

(C) He feels blue.

問題：這個男人覺得如何？

(A) 他覺得想睡覺。

(B) 他覺得很興奮。

(C) 他覺得很憂鬱。

Q3

Q: Lily bought two T-shirts. How much should she pay?

(A) Five hundred NT dollars.

(B) One hundred and five NT dollars.

(C) One thousand NT dollars.

問題：莉莉買了兩件 T 恤。她應該要付多少錢？

(A) 五百塊錢。

(B) 一百零五塊錢。

(C) 一千塊錢。

Q4

Q: What is the boy going to do?

(A) Go surfing.

(B) Go hiking.

(C) Go bowling.

問題：這個男孩將要做什麼？

(A) 去衝浪。

(B) 去登山健行。

(C) 去打保齡球。

Q5

Q: Now it's two thirty. What is Angela doing?

(A) Taking a bath.

(B) Playing the flute.

(C) Going to school.

問題：現在是兩點半。安琪拉正在做什麼？

(A) 洗澡。

(B) 吹笛子。

(C) 去上學。

學習成果測驗 PART 2 問答

Q1 Q: Is the coat on the couch yours?
(A) Yes, it's mine. Thanks.
(B) I have a heavy coat.
(C) There is a jacket on the couch.

問題：沙發上的外套是你的嗎？
(A) 是的，它是我的。謝謝。
(B) 我有一件大衣。
(C) 沙發上有一件夾克。

Q2 Q: It's so hot. Could you turn on the air conditioner?
(A) Sure. I also feel hot and stuffy.
(B) The air is fresh.
(C) Do you need some hot coffee?

問題：今天真熱。你能打開空調嗎？
(A) 當然。我也覺得又熱又悶。
(B) 空氣很新鮮。
(C) 你需要一些熱咖啡嗎？

Q3 Q: My phone number is 4255-8979.
(A) I don't have a cell phone.
(B) Pardon? Could you please say it again?
(C) Wow! It's cool.

問題：我的電話號碼是 4255-8979。
(A) 我沒有手機。
(B) 抱歉？你可以再說一次嗎？
(C) 哇！真酷。

Q4 Q: How often do you go to your grandma's house?
(A) On Sunday.
(B) After dinner.
(C) Twice a month.

  Ⓒ

問題：你多久去一次你奶奶家？
(A) 在週日。
(B) 在晚餐後。
(C) 一個月兩次。

Q5 Q: The train is leaving.
(A) I am coming.
(B) We are going to leave.
(C) Oh, no! I will miss the train.

問題：火車要離開了。
(A) 我來了。
(B) 我們要離開了。
(C) 哦，不！我會錯過這班火車

6 Q: It's raining!
(A) I have a lot of time.
(B) Yes, it's hot.
(C) Oh, no! Let's hurry up.

問題：下雨了！
(A) 我有很多時間。
(B) 是的，天氣很熱。
(C) 哦，不！我們快點。

7 Q: Where will you go after school?
(A) I was surfing on the Internet at that time.
(B) They will take a part-time job.
(C) We will go to the museum.

問題：你們放學後會去哪裡？
(A) 那時我正在瀏覽網路。
(B) 他們會接受兼差工作。
(C) 我們會去博物館。

8 Q: I don't feel well. I think I caught a cold.
(A) No, It's cool today.
(B) It's too bad.
(C) Take a rest and drink more water.

問題：我覺得不舒服。我想我感冒了。
(A) 不，今天很冷。
(B) 那太糟了。
(C) 休息一下，然後多喝點水。

9 Q: Here comes the bus 323. Oh, there are a lot of passengers in it!
(A) That's cool.
(B) I think we should wait for the next one.
(C) I need to go home.

問題：323號公車來了。哦，車廂裡有好多人！
(A) 那很酷。
(B) 我想我們應該要等下一班。
(C) 我得回家了。

10 Q: It's my new hat.
(A) Wow! It's pretty.
(B) I feel cold.
(C) We will go out.

問題：它是我的新帽子。
(A) 哇！它好漂亮。
(B) 我覺得冷。
(C) 我們會出去。

學習成果測驗 PART 3 簡短對話

Q1

M: I want to drive faster.
F: We can't. It's rush hour now.
M: Maybe we should take a detour.
F: Good idea.
Q: Why can't the man drive faster?
(A) because he is making a detour.
(B) because there are so many cars on the road.
(C) because the man and the woman are too busy.

男：我想開快一點。
女：我們不可以。現在是尖峰時間。
男：也許我們應該繞個路。
女：好主意。
問題：為什麼這個男人無法開快一點？
(A) 因為他正在繞路。
(B) 因為路上有好多的車子。
(C) 因為這個男人和女人太忙了。

Q2

F: Walk down this street until you get to Beauty Road.
M: How long will it take?
F: About five minutes.
M: Thank you very much.
Q: What does the man want to know?
(A) where he can buy a beautiful road.
(B) how long it will take to walk to Beauty Road.
(C) when he can walk.

女：往這條街下去直走，一直到美麗路。
男：要走多久？
女：大概五分鐘。
男：非常謝謝你。
問題：這個男的想知道什麼？
(A) 他可以在哪裡買到美麗路。
(B) 要多久才會走到美麗路。
(C) 他何時可以走路。

Q3

M: Good morning, Jane. Do you often go jogging in the morning?
F: No, it's my first time today. I want to lose some weight.
M: If you want to lose weight, you also should eat less.
F: Thank you for your suggestion.
Q: Where are the speakers?
(A) On the airplane
(B) In the restaurant
(C) In the park

男：早安，珍。你常常早上慢跑嗎？
女：不，今天是我的第一次。我想要減掉一些體重。
男：如果你想減重，你應該也要吃少一點
女：謝謝你的建議。
問題：說話者在哪裡？
(A) 在飛機上。
(B) 在餐廳裡。
(C) 在公園裡。

4 F: How old is your sister?
M: She's 5 years older than me.
F: How old are you?
M: 20 years old.
Q: How old is the man's sister?
(A) 10 years old
(B) 25 years old
(C) 5 years old

女：你姊姊多大？
男：她比我大五歲。
女：你幾歲？
男：二十歲。
問題：這個男人的姊姊幾歲？
(A) 十歲。
(B) 二十五歲。
(C) 五歲。

5 M: May I help you?
F: Yes, I'm looking for a kid's T-shirt for my son.
M: How tall is your son?
F: Around 120 cm tall.
Q: What is the woman doing?
(A) Buying some food for her son.
(B) Making a cake for her son.
(C) Buying the clothes for her son.

男：我能幫你嗎？
女：是的，我正在幫我兒子找一件 T 恤。
男：你兒子多高？
女：大約一百二十公分高。
問題：這個女人在做什麼？
(A) 幫他兒子買些食物。
(B) 幫她兒子做一個蛋糕。
(C) 幫她兒子買衣服。

6 M: May I help you?
F : I want two hamburgers and two cups of black tea.
M: Sorry, we don't have black tea. Do you want coffee?
F : Can I have two glasses of milk?
Q: Where is the woman?
(A) in the library
(B) at the hotel
(C) in the fast food restaurant

男：我能幫你嗎？
女：我想要兩個漢堡和兩杯紅茶。
男：抱歉，我們沒有紅茶。你想要咖啡嗎？
女：我能要兩杯牛奶嗎？
問題：這個女人在哪裡？
(A) 在圖書館。
(B) 在旅館。
(C) 在速食餐廳。

Q7
B: Mom, what should I do first?
W: Clean the window first, and then help me mop the floor.
B: OK.
W: Hey, come here to help me move the sofa. I need to sweep the floor.
Q: What are the speakers doing?
(A) Cleaning the house.
(B) Moving the tables.
(C) Watching TV.

男：媽媽，我應該先做什麼？
女：先清理窗戶，然後幫我拖地板。
男：好的。
女：嘿，過來這裡幫我搬一下這個沙發。我需要掃地。
問題：說話者在做什麼？
(A) 清理房子。
(B) 移動餐桌。
(C) 看電視。

Q8
M: Hello, can I speak to Helen?
W: Sorry, she's not at home. Who is calling?
M: This is Tom. I'm her colleague. Could you tell her to call me back?
W: OK. I'll tell her. Bye!
Q: What do we learn from the conversation?
(A) Helen and Tom work together.
(B) Helen is talking on the phone.
(C) Tom and Helen live together.

男：哈囉，我可以跟海倫說話嗎？
女：抱歉，她不在家。哪位打來？
男：我是湯姆。我是她的同事。可以請你訴她回電話給我嗎？
女：好的，我會跟她說。再見！
問題：我們從這個對話中得知什麼？
(A) 海倫和湯姆一起工作。
(B) 海倫正在講電話。
(C) 湯姆和海倫住在一起。

Q9
W: There is a seat.
M: Thank you. It's kind of you to give me your seat.
W: Don't mention it!
M: God will bless you.
Q: Where are the speakers?
(A) In the men's room.
(B) On the bus
(C) In the river.

女：那裡有個位子。
男：謝謝。你真好心給我一個位子。
女：別客氣！
男：上帝會保祐你的。
問題：說話者在哪裡？
(A) 在男廁。
(B) 在公車上。
(C) 在河裡。

Ⓐ  

10 M: How are you today?
F : It's just not my day.
M: Cheer up! Everything will be fine.
F : Thanks.
Q: Which one is TRUE?
(A) The woman feels bad.
(B) The woman doesn't have a day.
(C) The man is sad.

男：你今天如何？
女：今天很倒楣。
男：振作起來！事情會好轉的。
女：謝謝。
問題：哪一個是真的？
(A) 這個女人覺得很糟。
(B) 這個女人沒有日子。
(C) 這個男人很傷心。

學習成果測驗 PART 4 短文聽解

01 Please look at the following three pictures.
Julia left a message on Wendy's answering machine. How will Wendy go to New York?
Hello, Wendy. This is Julia. Bill and I are happy that you are coming tomorrow. Your flight will arrive at New York Airport at five thirty in the evening, right? We will go to pick you up. It is chilly and snowy here, so you must bring a heavy coat with you. See you tomorrow.
請看以下的三張圖片。
茱莉亞在溫蒂的答錄機裡留了一則留言。溫蒂會如何去紐約？
哈囉，溫蒂。我是茱莉亞。比爾和我很高興你明天要來。你的班機會在傍晚五點半抵達紐約機場是嗎？我們會去接你。這裡又冷又下雪，所以你得帶一件大外套。明天見。

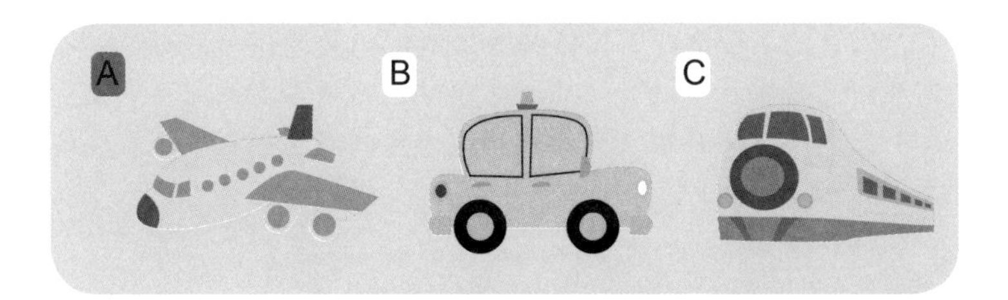

Q2 Please look at the following three pictures.
Chris left this message in Sarah's voice mailbox. When will everyone meet?
Hello, Sarah. The date and time of the party has actually been changed. Instead of going o
tomorrow night, we decided to meet tonight at seven o'clock. I know I'm telling you this a litt
late, but the other guys just told me about the change one hour ago. I hope you can meet u
tonight.
請看以下的三張圖片。
克里斯在莎拉的語音信箱裡留了一則訊息。大家何時會見面？
哈囉，莎拉。派對的日期和時間真的改了。我們決定今晚七點鐘見面，而不是明天晚上再出去
我知道現在告訴你這個有點晚了，但其他人也都是在一個鐘頭前才告訴我改時間的這件事。我
望你今晚可以和我們見面。

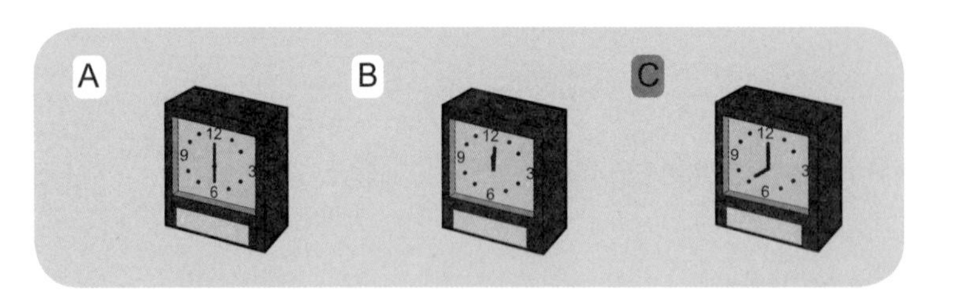

Q3 Please look at the following three pictures.
Greg wrote a text message to one of his employees. What is the worst thing that Greg
employee did?
When you are in meetings, do not eat potato chips anymore. When I am talking, I don't want
hear the loud sound of crunching. Even worse, you left your trash in the meeting room on th
table. Please remember that we don't have any cleaning ladies to pick up the office, so if yo
forget to pick up your garbage, I have to do it.
請看以下的三張圖片。
葛瑞格寫了一則簡訊給他其中一位員工。什麼是葛瑞格的員工所做的最糟的一件事？
當你在會議室時，不要再吃洋芋片。當我在說話時，我不希望聽到咔啦咔啦的聲音。更糟的是
你把你的垃圾留在會議室的桌子上。請記得我們沒有打掃的太太幫我們整理辦公室，所以如果
忘了清理垃圾，我就得去清理。

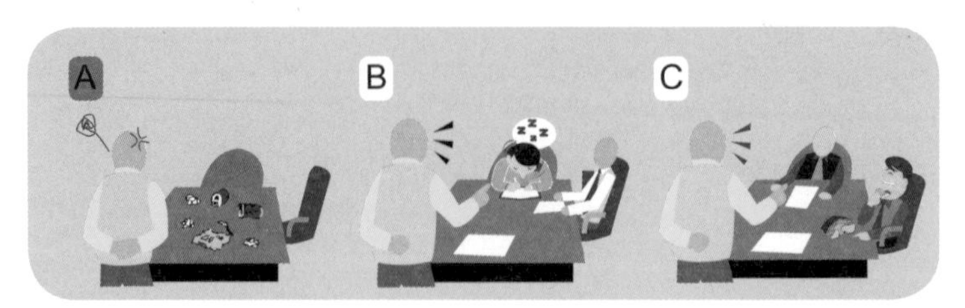

Q4 Please look at the following three pictures.
Fred left a message on Betty's answering machine. Where will Fred go after school today?
Hello, Betty, this is Fred. Jessica told me that you are sick. Do you feel better now? Did you see a doctor? Jessica and I are going to visit you after school in the afternoon. Do we need to bring anything for you?
請看以下的三張圖片。
佛瑞德在貝蒂的答錄機上留了一則留言。佛瑞德今天放學後會去哪裡？
哈囉，貝蒂，我是佛瑞德。潔西卡告訴我你生病了。你現在有覺得好一點嗎？你有去看醫生嗎？潔西卡和我今天下午放學後會去看你。你需要我們幫你帶些什麼東西嗎？

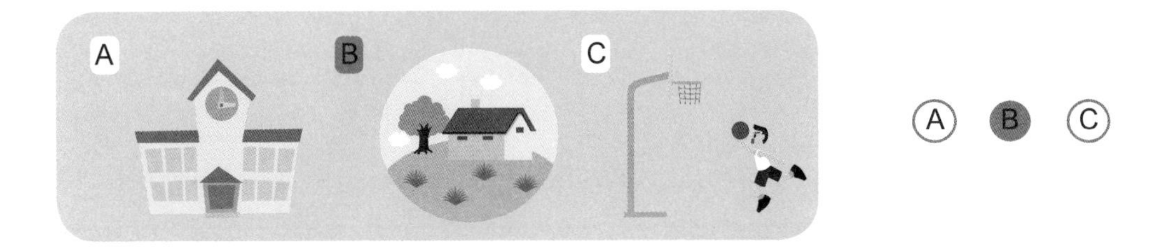

Q5 Please look at the following three pictures.
Listen to the following short talk. What does Kelly have for lunch every day?
Kelly is on a diet. She goes jogging every morning and then just eats an egg and drinks a glass of juice for breakfast. At noon, she has salad and a glass of milk in the office. After work, she eats some fruit for dinner, and then takes a walk for one hour.
請看以下的三張圖片。
注意聽接下來的短文。凱莉每天午餐都吃些什麼？
凱莉在節食。她每天早上去慢跑，接著只吃一個雞蛋和喝一杯果汁當早餐。中午時，她在辦公室吃沙拉和喝一杯牛奶。下班後，她吃一些水果當晚餐，接著她會去散步一個小時。

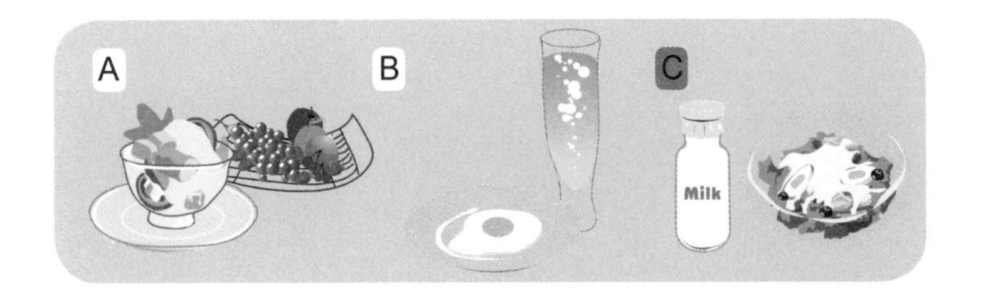

國家圖書館出版品預行編目(CIP)資料

初級聽力 STARTER / 徐薇編著. -- 臺北市：碩英,
2012.06
面；公分
ISBN 978-986-88417-0-3(平裝附光碟片)
1. 英語 2. 問題集
805.1892 101010866

初級聽力 *Starter*

編著：徐薇
責任編輯：賴依寬、黃怡欣、黃思瑜
美術編輯：蔡佳容、陳爾筠
錄音製作：風華錄音室
行銷企劃：凃聖敏
發行人：江正明
發行公司：碩英出版社
地址：106 台北市大安區安和路二段 70 號 2 樓之 3
電話：02-2708-5508
傳真：02-2707-1669
本版發行日：2012 年 6 月
定價：NT$ 300